A House for Her

and Other Stories

By

Dene Hellman

Gathered Thoughts Books
Published by Indigo Sea Press
Winston-Salem

Gathered Thoughts Books
Indigo Sea Press
PO Box 67201
Winston-Salem, NC 27114

First Gathered Thoughts Books edition published April, 2017
Gathered Thoughts Books, Moon Sailor and all production design are trademarks of Indigo Sea Press, used under license.

Cover illustrations courtesy *State Center, Iowa Archives, I & II*, Walsworth Publishing, 2003

For information regarding bulk purchases of this book, digital purchase and special discounts, please contact the publisher at indigoseapress@gmail.com

Cover Concept by Dene Hellman
Cover design by Pan Morelli
Manufactured in the United States of America
ISBN 978-1-63066-465-7

For my mother,

Margaretta Damman Grew,

who taught me that we are surrounded by stories.

Acknowledgements

Most of us are aware of twists and turns in the lives of the people around us. Without being gossips or encouraging that trait in others, we laugh, cry, and share concerns with them. Some of the best memories I have of my mother are times when the two of us did the dinner dishes together and discussed the latest in town or school happenings. Often, her laughter would ring out, strong and free. She had a lot of things to do and to worry about but our "story time" was a respite.

My thanks go to a lot of people who have helped move the tales of *A House for Her* from conception to publication. First of all, one needs a "first reader," someone who reads one's initial writing and gives an honest assessment, no holds barred. This time, my daughter, Patricia Bartholomew, was that first reader and she has my extreme gratitude for sharing her thoughts about what worked and what didn't, all the while encouraging my efforts and providing additional insights.

Additional thanks go to Grandson Travis DeBacker, who took time from his busy schedule to read the reworked stories of *A House for Her*. They benefitted from his suggestions, insights, and attention to detail. An astute reader, Travis made a tremendous difference that will stay with me in my ongoing writing.

A big "thank you" goes to Shirley Schaper of State Center, Iowa, for permission to use collected and published State Center photos as part of the cover design. Thanks to the town of State Center, as well. It is a small, beautiful place with a long history going back to pioneer days.

As always, my appreciation and thanks go to Mike Simpson of Indigo Sea Publishing, whose patience and insight give the telling of stories a happy outcome.

Table of Contents

Part One
A Shadow Chorus

MOTHER CAT

OUR CAT WAS A SLUT, as country cats often are.

Well, anyway, that's what my mother called her when our semi-pet had one litter of kittens after another. This was back in the day, when people weren't as into their animals as they are now and certainly didn't go running to a veterinarian with them for all manner of shots, surgeries, or—heaven forbid—*dental care.*

But there were, even then, a few people who chose to curb their pets' offspring bearing and they took them to the local animal doctor. I doubt he considered the task a valuable part of his practice, preferring to administer to "worthwhile" animals like cows, pigs and horses, but he didn't get to be one of the most prosperous people in the community by turning down jobs. My friend Betty wasn't sure what was done in these medical interventions, even though she was the veterinarian's daughter, but must have heard the term "spaying" because she would explain that people brought their pets to her father to be "spaded" so they wouldn't have puppies or kittens. She also informed me that her family's dog, an overweight and unappealing terrier named "Queenie," had been spaded.

When our house cat went into one of the periodic yowling spells that announced her wish to copulate, Mother would take her out to the barn and shut her in, theoretically to keep her from being violated by tom cats. The toms got in anyway and in a couple of months here would come another batch of kittens.

Consequently, my poor father would time and again be instructed to take all the newly born kittens and do away with them, a task he hated. I think he took the still-blind bits of feline new borns, stuck them in a burlap bag, and drowned them. My everlasting hope that I'd be allowed to keep a kitten was always disappointed.

1

"Aw, Madge!" Father would say, "Would it hurt to let her have one?"

Eventually, our cat disappeared. She may have succumbed to one of the wild life species that roamed the countryside. A hawk—a coyote—a raccoon: it was the law of the land that animals were part of a vast and merciless food chain. Our cat wasn't the end of it, of course. She caught mice, the task for which she was tolerated in the first place.

Only I, it seemed, felt true affection for her and only I went around looking after she disappeared. As a family, we never took on another pet.

Two and a half decades later, all manner of things were changing. There was the matter of wars: we couldn't get enough of them, it seemed to my non-political self.

Women's roles began to be weighed, and about time. Betty, who would have been a great animal doctor had she gone through veterinary medicine studies and joined her father in practice, had instead been sent to an upscale girls' college to learn social niceties. She went on to marry a pharmacist, have two children and do volunteer work on Monday and Friday mornings in the library.

With no money or aspirations for my future in my background, student loans unknown, and few scholarships yet available for women, I had managed a few courses in office skills at a so-called business college and ended up in a not-too-bad job as the office manager of a vegetable canning association.

Eventually, I settled down in the same house where I'd grown up. Mother and Father didn't need it anymore; they had, individually, succumbed to cancer and passed on. God knows, I had very little sentimentality about the place but enjoyed remodeling it and creating a tenant apartment in the barn—doing most of the physical labor myself, as a matter of fact. Earning a man's wages in the office was not going to happen but at home I could do whatever I was capable of and who could argue?

Not attracted to the idea of marriage, I invited my close friend, Sheila, to move in with me. That she did, for reasons that were ours alone.

Lesbians—a word some people had never heard—were not yet an acknowledged part of small town society so women like us who chose to live together in domestic comfort did so under the umbrella of fiscal convenience. As women, our salaries were meager and it was not difficult for people to consider that shared expenses were a sufficient rationale for a couple of women to split a household. Additionally, we retained respectability by continuing to sing in our church choir and volunteering to do fund collections for March of Dimes.

Living happily ever after, the time came when Sheila and I decided to adopt a pet and put in a request for one of the kittens that a colleague of hers anticipated. We'd met the nicely pedigreed expectant mother and pronounced it beautiful and charming. It was the first and only litter she would be allowed before a trip to the veterinarian to "fix" her. We'd adopt one of the males after it was weaned and name him something clever that we had not yet formulated.

However, before all that could come to pass, a kitten adopted *us*. Unlike our friend's cat, it had no pedigree or familial beauty to draw upon, nor did it display the kind of obsequious attention that makes for bonding between animal and adopting family. It simply showed up in the barn one morning when I was finishing up some gardening chores. When I went to put the lawnmower away, I saw a shadowy form skitter behind a pile of rakes and shovels. I later mentioned as much to Sheila and she went to investigate. She came into the kitchen a half hour later with the kitten gripped in her hand. It was mewing frantically and trying to get away—to what we couldn't imagine. It was semi-scrawny and its short grey coat verged on being tattered. For sure, it was nobody's escaped pet and something bad may have happened to its mother because it hardly looked old enough to have been weaned.

Sheila was enchanted and ran to fill a saucer with milk. She put the kitten down in front of the saucer, where it lapped away for a period of time before, satiated, it collapsed on one of the braided rugs Sheila cherished for its pedigree as handmade in the Amana colonies. Sheila picked it up, rug and all, and transferred it to a warmed bath towel that could be tucked around its sleeping form. Gently lowering herself into a rocking chair, she sat holding that kitten for the better part of two hours and when she got to her feet she and the kitten were as one.

3

"It's a girl," I said, when I managed a close look.

"Let's find a cute name for her," Sheila said, hardly breathing. "Chris, we *are* going to keep her, aren't we? After all, *she* came to *us!*"

I don't remember what name we came up with. Something saccharine, like "Princess" or "Missy," as I recall, neither of which was very appropriate and certainly not answered to by the kitten. Perhaps its name was "Sweetheart," since that's how Sheila always addressed it. I was more likely to refer to the kitten as "it." As it grew, it was tolerant of Sheila's endearments but came to me only when it wanted to be fed or have a door opened and Sheila wasn't nearby. From the start, it had no interest in using a litter box and would simply stand by the back door when it wanted to go outdoors to tend to its various kinds of business. It had other characteristics, as well, including a tendency to follow us around when we were involved in housekeeping chores, inside or out.

One day when I was home and Sheila was still at her bookkeeping job in the local hospital, the cat followed me out to the barn. I was putting the finishing touches on the small apartment that we optimistically thought would provide us with some additional income. As I washed the new kitchen sink and probed into the corners of newly installed cabinets, I noticed the kitten, by now half grown, was sitting very still in the middle of the room, watching my every move. Ordinarily, I wouldn't have paid much attention, but her wide-eyed gaze began to look familiar—and not familiar in a particularly pleasant way. She was, in fact, looking at me with the kind of critical observation that my mother used to direct at me every time I made a move either physically or verbally.

"Madge!" I said to her. Madge had been my mother's name and its one-syllable, exclamatory sound fit our cat exactly. It would have been too flaky of me to address the cat as "Mother" but Madge was surely allowable.

The cat accepted the name with a movement that was eerily like a shrug and I understood why she was watching me. Hadn't she always (when she really was my mother)? She would have thought my housekeeping chores were done in a less than satisfactory way or that I wasn't being sufficiently attentive to the other tasks waiting my attention and would have let me know about it—by a look if

4

nothing else. In the present case, she likely would have thought me lax for not using a disinfectant on the sink.

When Sheila got home, I was in the kitchen getting dinner and Madge was watching from the dining room door. I explained that our feline friend liked being called Madge and Sheila was skeptical about it but agreeable. I did *not* tell her that Madge was the reincarnation of my mother. Sheila went on addressing her as "Sweetheart" and the three of us settled into a routine wherein the two of them were happy with their relationship and Madge, the cat, continued communicating to me that I could surely do things better if I tried harder.

When Madge was about seven or eight months old, she set up a caterwauling that was all too familiar. It was, in a way, the dreaded sound of my childhood: the announcement that a cat wished to mate. Madge was good at it and an excellent advertisement for the vitamins Sheila poured into her; she yowled and shrieked beyond anyone's capacity to tolerate the sound.

"My God!" screamed Sheila. "What's wrong with her? She must be sick! I've never heard anything like it!"

I tried to be objective in my answer. "Uh, don't worry, Sheila. It's just Nature making itself obvious. Madge wants to mate and have kittens and we just can't let that happen."

Madge went on screeching around the house, furiously making her biology known to us, and we did our best to ignore it while also ignoring her wishes to get outside. In fact, it seemed to me that she was getting her comeuppance in this life for what she'd done in her last. I wasn't about to take her out and shut her in the barn to yowl her frustrations alone, and instead endured her traumas with a certain amount of inner satisfaction.

She stopped, at last, and I knew the obvious rationale of the next step. Madge would have to be fixed/neutered/spayed (spaded, if you will). I was adamant about it and Sheila was semi-horrified but resigned. Madge sat looking at me with those Mother eyes, as in, "You are, of course, making a wretched decision about me. I am at your mercy, but the time will come when you will regret it!"

When we brought her home from the veterinarian, Madge fixed me with another accusatory stare and then went on about her business, as I knew she would; the Madges of the world are not much slowed down by sentimentality.

We rented the new apartment to a genial man named Hank who was freshly divorced, in his thirties, and drove a fork lift at good wages for a local business. Hank was pretty much an ideal tenant, considerate of our privacy, clean, and prompt with rent. He was also tolerant of Madge and allowed her to visit whenever he was home. The apartment had a nice big kitchen window with a sunny exposure and it was her pleasure to sprawl in the rays of light that fell across the floor.

She may have liked our renter but didn't expand her tolerance to include our women acquaintances. We saw evidence of that one evening when Sheila and I entertained our church circle. There Madge sat, mid-living room, as our guests came through the front door, her body language saying, "I don't like this one little bit!" She had matured into quite a nice looking cat, thanks to good nutrition and the first-class grooming she received from Sheila, but her attitude toward outsiders was snotty. Now, she was all set to keep an eye on these interlopers, despite their flattering comments about her.

"Just take your coats back to Sheila's room," I instructed everyone. This was a bit of fiction, since Sheila and I shared the big bedroom. However, Sheila kept her clothes and a few personal items in the other bedroom for convenience's sake and also had spiced it up with some of her family photos and artifacts. She was very much into the decorating style called "Early American" and no real or pseudo antique escaped her admiration. Visitors wouldn't doubt that she slept in the single bed so sweetly covered with one of her grandmother's finest quilts. It was camouflage, pure and simple.

Madge certainly must have understood that, but sulked as the women entered, laid their coats on the bed, and cooed over one or another of Sheila's personal touches. She demonstrated her disdain when one of the women, a nice enough lady who fancied herself as a cat lover, bent over to scratch her on the head.

Chomp went her teeth on the poor woman's extended fingers. The victim screamed, whereupon Madge darted under the bed. There was blood, of course—not much, but skin was broken and it took many, many apologies, the application of a Band Aid, and Sheila's dedicated attention for the rest of the evening before the event was smoothed over.

After everyone, at last, went home, Sheila cried. Madge had

crawled out from under the bed and Sheila said, over and over again, "Sweetheart, how could you do such a thing?"

I waited until later, when Sheila was in the bathroom getting ready for bed, to address the problem. I found Madge in the kitchen finishing up the remains of her dinner. Relentlessly, I swooped down and took her dish away from her. Holding it in my hand, I confronted our wayward cat.

"Listen here, Madge," I said. "You know damn well that what you did tonight was uncalled for. I'm not particularly happy about having outsiders in our house either, but sometimes we have to put up with it. If you ever, EVER bite anybody again, you can bid goodbye to your nice comfy lifestyle. Out to the barn you'll go and that's where you'll stay!"

I put the dish down and Madge finished her meal but for weeks afterward she wore a moderately chastened look. Whenever someone stopped by, a church member or someone else from the community, she would give me one of her frozen Madge stares, then arrogantly stick her tail straight up in the air and retreat behind the sofa or into a distant corner of the pantry. It worked for both of us.

Hank continued to be an ideal tenant so we wished him all good things and also hoped he wouldn't get remarried any time soon. Once in a while I noticed him casting an appreciative glance toward Sheila, who was definitely cute, but he may have had some understanding of the relationship she and I shared because he never followed his glances up by asking her out. After a few months, he began sporadically dating some of the local women but didn't invite them over to his apartment. We hadn't said he shouldn't but appreciated his consideration.

That consideration made it harder when, in the spring, he finally did get around to asking us for a favor. He belonged to the National Guard and was due for a three-week training period elsewhere in the state. He said he had a younger brother, Perrin, a truck driver who was temporarily at loose ends. Hank didn't explain Perrin's "loose ends" but said his brother would like to live in Hank's apartment while he was away. Would that be okay with us?

We didn't give it much consideration. Sheila said, "Hank is so nice I can't imagine anybody else in his family not being just as pleasant."

Dene Hellman

I tended to agree with her assessment. Madge was, of course, uninterested. Why wouldn't she assume that Hank's brother would also welcome her into the apartment to share its kitchen sunlight? All three of us had our assumptions thwarted. When Hank brought Perrin over to meet us, his brother turned out to be Hank's opposite in many respects, one of those cases when one wonders if they really do share family ties.

Hank had a plain Midwestern accent but spoke in courteous tones as befit a well-raised person; Perrin had the voice and attitude of someone raised behind a seedy bar—a bar frequented by illiterates who tried to out-yell one another and peppered their speech with obscenities.

Hank dressed like any workman but his clothes always looked fresh and as if he'd taken a stab at them with an iron; Perrin's clothes looked as if they'd been washed not more recently than a couple of weeks ago and, for sure, had never seen an iron.

Hank said that he was sure appreciative that we had agreed to Perrin being around for the next few weeks; Perrin turned his head away at that, hawked and spat, missing Madge by only a few inches.

Within days, we saw that Perrin never opened the blinds on his windows, that his garbage, mostly empty beer and cola cans, piled up outside his door instead of being carried over to our trash barrels. Additionally, he played music that thumped and shrieked at a fever pitch into the wee hours of the night and yelled at Madge to get lost whenever she presented herself at his door.

We looked at the calendar and wondered if we could be polite through the remaining two weeks of his residency. We also decided that if Hank, when he returned, wanted to continue sharing his apartment with Perrin, we would have to decline permission even if it meant losing Hank as a renter.

Temporarily ignoring the situation didn't work. Twice, Perrin called us on the apartment telephone—once to say the toilet was stopped up and once to claim we must be holding his mail because he hadn't had any since moving in.

The mail complaint was invalid. We had rural delivery because we were outside city limits and nothing with Perrin's name on it had been left in our box; Hank had his own box in the local post office and picked his mail up when he was in town. I reported this and was answered with something close to a snarl before the man slammed the phone down without offering a "thanks anyway"—a routine response taught by all small town families to be used when a request has been declined. I reflected again on how he and Hank could possibly have the same mother.

In the case of the stopped-up toilet, ordinarily I would, as soon as possible, have gone out to the apartment to see what I could do— but not this time. I called Roger at the local hardware who sometimes did odd handyman jobs.

"Ya break your arm?" he jokingly said. Guys I'd known all my life knew there wasn't much they could do that I couldn't do. I'd gained my reputation early—by playing high school basketball so well that our team went to State Finals and then scored enough points to put our town over the top. A lifetime of local reverence was my payback.

"Well," I said, "Hank is letting his brother use his apartment for a couple of weeks and there's something about this guy that I don't care for. Besides, I'd probably have a shit fit if I saw the state of the bathroom and end up throwing him out. Do me a favor?"

Enough said. Roger came out to the apartment and reported back to me when I got home from work. "Chris, you're right about the state of the bathroom. It's a pigsty. However, nothing wrong with the toilet. We sold you a good one and you installed it right. It looks like it's being used to wash muddy boots but the water still goes out and comes in the way it's supposed to. I never seen that Perrin jerk before. I bet he was just trying to get you or Sheila out to the apartment so he could stir up trouble."

The following weekend Perrin had a party. Cars came and went most of the night, their drivers probably drunk because they deliberately ran their vehicles over our lawn with radios blaring and spotlights shining in our windows.

On Monday morning, calling from my cannery office, I reached Perrin on the apartment phone.

"You've overstepped our hospitality and, probably, Hank's. I want you out of the apartment tomorrow, if not today. If you don't comply, I'll bring charges against you," was the essence of my message.

Obviously, Perrin was sleeping off his weekend, because he

didn't argue, managing only to mutter, "I hear 'ya," before hanging up.

The next day, a Tuesday, I pleaded business needs and stayed home from work. The morning was uneventful. The presence of Perrin's pickup said he was still in the apartment and I wondered if I'd have to call the sheriff to back up my threats. Then, around 2:00 I saw him bring a few things out of the apartment to stow in his truck. Actually, he brought out more things than we'd observed him carrying in and I crossed my fingers that he wasn't helping himself to Hank's possessions. He took his time and seemed to be in a calm frame of mind. After the truck was loaded, he went back inside and my sense of what was proper told me that he was surely tidying up the apartment, the decent thing to do before its return to Hank.

Around 4:00, Perrin walked up on our back porch. When I answered the inside door to his loud knock, he shouted, "Hey, I'm returnin' the apartment key!" He waved it in the air and, against my better judgment, I unlocked and opened the storm door.

Quickly, so fast that he must have had his moves planned, he inserted his foot between it and me and forced his way into the kitchen. I took a couple of steps back, ready to defend myself if necessary, but instinct was no match for his thought-out assault. I'm strong but he was stronger and at well over six feet and 200 pounds, he quickly had my arms pinned. A few quick twists on his part and both were out of commission. As it turned out, he broke one of them, as well as the wrist on the other arm. Then he knocked my legs out from under me and succeeded in breaking one of those by accurately aiming a heavily shod foot to the knee. As a last precaution against my ability to act, he slammed me in the mouth with his doubled fist.

Unctuously, without a show of anger, he purred, "That'll show you two fairies what a real man can do! You can lay there and think about it while we wait. I'm conservin' my strength for your little girlfriend. Then I'll get back to you so you won't be disappointed."

With that, he maneuvered himself to the back of the kitchen, close to the dining room and out of view of anyone coming up on the porch.

I looked at the clock. Sheila often got home from her hospital shift about now. Likely, our schedule had been under Perrin's scrutiny since he'd moved in, lending deliberation to the fantasies of the brute. I was out of commission, physically, and my pain was bad enough to cause distortion of thought. Basically, I wanted to kill the guy and would have done so if I had been capable of getting at him.

Turning my head to one side, I saw Madge huddled in the side pantry, where she often went to avoid visitors. She was studying me with eyes that were surprisingly wide with fear and concern. I nodded at her, hoping she'd stay well out of sight through whatever misery Perrin had planned for Sheila and me.

The clock ticked and my heart raced—not for myself but for Sheila. When her footsteps sounded on the porch, I tried to scream a warning but found that I couldn't. Perrin had finished incapacitating me when he smashed me in the mouth.

Just as Sheila made a step into the kitchen, he made it across the room and grabbed her. Not willing to leave his behavior to her imagination, he repeated what he'd said to me. "You two fairies need a lesson. Nothin' to compare with a good man, and I'm here to demonstrate that to your heart's content! Give me trouble and I'll do you like I did your tough little friend there!" He nodded in my direction and Sheila gasped in horror and fear.

Just as he pressed his mouth down on Sheila's, holding her arms locked behind her back, I saw Madge creep across the floor. Suddenly, without a sound, she flew through the air, hurling herself at Perrin and sinking her sharp, young feline teeth into his arm. Her claws went out and attached themselves to his chest and back. He yelled and tried to shake her off but failed. Essentially, he was *wearing* that cat and she wasn't going to let go no matter what.

Sheila was fast. The action was happening next to the kitchen stove and she took advantage of her assailant's temporary lapse by reaching over and grabbing the heavy cast iron frying pan that was a permanently displayed testimony to her Early American decorating tastes. Adrenalin saturated, she swung it hard against Perrin's head, then against his shoulder. He went down on the floor, unconscious from the blows, and Madge let loose of his arm and backed off.

Sheila burst into tears and bent over me, trying to find out how much I'd been hurt. I nodded toward the telephone that hung on the kitchen wall and she said, "Oh, of course!" and called for emergency help. Then she picked up the iron frying pan again and stood over

Perrin, ready to bash him in the head once more if he regained consciousness.

Both Perrin and I were taken to the local hospital in ambulances. It was going to take me a good while to get mended and recover my strength but Perrin was in far worse shape. He was in a coma and it would take him nearly a month to wake up; as a weapon of choice, a cast iron frying pan was pretty lethal.

As soon as he was able to navigate he was carted off to jail.

It turned out that he wasn't really Hank's brother; he was a cousin that Hank felt sorry for even though he didn't know him well. Hank's mother, a sister of Perrin's mother, had put pressure on Hank to "help Perrin have a second chance" after her nephew got out of his latest jail term for an assortment of crimes, including theft and rape.

"He just didn't get raised right," she said. "His step dad was always mean to him and my sister was scared to death to get in the way 'cause he wasn't beyond beating her up, too."

A dutiful son, Hank had complied with his mother's wishes. He apologized and apologized to Sheila and me and knew enough to move out of our apartment immediately.

It wasn't livable anyway; Perrin had thoroughly wrecked it. He likely had made use of the two hours he spent after loading his truck by trashing everything in sight. The toilet was stuffed with debris until it overflowed, the doors of the kitchen appliances and cupboards were torn off their hinges, all window shades were pulled off and slashed with a knife, leftover paint stashed in a back closet had been dragged out and poured over the floor coverings. And, predictably, Hank's television and record player, as well as most of his winter clothes, had been loaded into the pickup to be taken wherever Perrin was going next.

We had insurance that covered some of the damage but not all, and it would be several months before I was healed enough to begin repairs. We weren't surprised to learn that Perrin would now be sent up for a very long time. Sheila and I had been lucky to escape the worst and hoped he wouldn't be eligible for parole for years and years. As it turned out, a year later he got into a knife fight in the prison dining room and was killed—thereby causing us to feel relieved when we knew we should instead entertain feelings of pity.

Madge went around looking even more complacent than usual. She knew that I wasn't going to banish her to the barn for her attack on Perrin and took advantage of both Sheila and me, translating our gratitude to her into fancier food and a sincere welcome to the warmest spot in the house—which happened to be our bed. Sheila said, "Doesn't she just have the cutest little purr?" I could have missed it but knew better than to offend two-thirds of the household by saying so.

The identity that looked out of Madge's eyes, the part that was my mother, began to mellow and at last went away altogether.

MRS. WESTFIELD

ARRIVING AT HOME AFTER her American Association of University Women meeting, Mrs. Westfield headed straight for the powder room situated off the back hall. Tripping the commode handle shortly thereafter, she briefly watched the water swirl around and down the immaculate fixture and then turned her attention to washing her hands the recommended length of time required to sing *Happy birthday to You!* Twice.

It hadn't been a particularly pleasant evening. The guest speaker's presentation did not reflect thorough research and Tricia Mosley, at whose home the meeting was held, was not a great hostess. "Careless," is how Mrs. Westfield described it to herself. Mrs. Westfield's tea cup had had a discernible chip near the handle. It belonged to a set of Spode that Tricia had inherited from her maternal family that was no doubt revered; nevertheless, the cup should have been retired from active duty.

Little mistakes like that were immediately taken care of in the Westfield household. Plus, anything she didn't happen to notice would be called to her attention immediately by Janette, her household helper of many years.

Mrs. Westfield now thought about Janette and, as always, gave thanks for her to the deity to whom she directed her more sanctified thoughts. Janette had been part of her household, three days a week, fifty weeks a year, for just about twenty years. Well paid by domestic help standards and much appreciated, Janette had long ago given up the other household for which she worked. She had plenty to do at her own home, first with her young children, then with the greater challenges that came as they matured. Better, she said, to scrimp a little than be gone from home where God only knew what went on in her absence.

The two women, Janette and Mrs. Westfield, got along very well. If Mrs. Westfield was a tiny bit obsessive - compulsive, Janette seemed just about as equally so as her employer. Together, they kept an impeccable home that was ready for viewing any day of the week at any time. The curtains were as dust-free as the dining room table. The kitchen floor was as flawlessly smudge-free as the bathroom lavatory. The window panes sparkled as brightly as the silverware nested in its velvet-lined compartments.

Janette was, in fact, so appreciated by Mrs. Westfield that the later would gladly have cut her a good bit of slack. Certainly, she would have been content to let her forego the gray uniform and uber-respectful manner. Over their twenty-year association, she even suggested that Janette address her as "Martha." From time to time she invited her out to lunch at places that she believed Janette would enjoy, but Janette always went on calling her "Mrs. Westfield," stuck to the gray uniform, and found puzzling excuses to avoid being a luncheon guest.

Mrs. Westfield was no snob and Janette's reserve hurt her feelings. Occasionally, she wondered if she expected too much. She had been raised to want her surroundings to be perfect but that wasn't, she thought, a bad thing. It was reassuring that Janette seemed to have the same standards. Although Janette offered little information about her own family, Mrs. Westfield assumed all was well.

Widowed after several decades of a good marriage, Mrs. Westfield went on doing what she did best—acting as hostess for the events, committee meetings and celebrations of the five groups in which she was involved. True, sometimes the AAUW, as tonight, met in other members' homes, as did the book club, the symphony orchestra's auxiliary, the Altar Society, and the travel club in which both she and her husband had been active. But none of these meetings ever went as well as they did when held in the Westfield home. Moreover, all of the organizations' members knew that she didn't need much advance notice to welcome any and all varieties of get-togethers. Her house was, without exception, spotless. Plus — this was crucial—refreshments always seemed to materialize at her fingertips. Reluctant and ill-prepared hostesses counted on it, often calling members at the last minute to announce that an unforeseeable emergency had arisen but Martha Westfield would graciously pinch-hit.

It was a shock when Janette didn't show up one Tuesday morning, the very day when the travel society was to meet at the Westfield residence to see a film about India.

Travel society meetings were a lot of work because they

included those husbands who were still alive and healthy. Extra seating and heartier food were needed. Chairs had to be brought from the basement and substitutes found for the little sandwiches and tea cookies that were usual at women's gatherings. Mrs. Westfield definitely could not do all of that by herself, which Janette well knew, so her absence—minus an explanatory phone call—was worrisome. The only possible justification was that Janette was sick. In twenty years, Mrs. Westfield had never been invited to Janette's home and she would never have dreamed of intruding on her assistant's privacy. Now, however, she got into her car and programmed Janette's address into the direction finder. It led her into an unfamiliar part of town where, apparently, no member of any of her five organizations lived.

The Voice finally announced "1146 is on the left."

This was Janette's house? It was small and looked discouraged in a number of ways. A large boxwood that grew beside the front door was long overdue for clipping and a grimy lawnmower stood abandoned in the midst of a now-overgrown lawn. There was no evidence of Janette's compulsive tidiness, the trait that had strengthened the bond between employer and helper.

Ascending the porch carefully, Mrs. Westfield called Janette's name and added, "Are you okay?"

A Janette she didn't know, sans gray uniform, hair in disarray, answered the call, opening the door with unwelcoming body language.

"I thought you might be sick and need help," Mrs. Westfield said. "It worried me when you didn't call or show up this morning."

"No time to call," said Janette, "and didn't even think of it. You got to learn to get along without help. My own daughter needs me and next month I'm eligible to go on Social Security."

She nodded toward two children who were sitting much too close to a television set. A younger child crawled across a sofa, one hand gripping a disintegrating sandwich from which dribbled peanut butter and jelly. The sofa, Mrs. Westfield noted, was a sad contrast to her own immaculate couch that was kept nicely vacuumed and plumped by the very Janette who now stood defiantly before her.

"My daughter had her kids taken away from her," Janette said, with no hint of embarrassment. "The baby is in a foster home right now," she added. "He's going to be living here after next week. I got no time to look after you and your little pretend parties."

Hurt to the quick, Mrs. Westfield nevertheless lived up to the person she was to the core of her being. "I am so sorry for your troubles," she said. "Let me help," she added.

Although she had scrupulously paid into Social Security on Janette's behalf, the Social Security that would now play such an important role in Janette's finances, she realized with sudden insight that during the twenty years of Janette's services she had given no thought to a retirement plan for her. While she occasionally sent thought waves of appreciation toward her late husband and his careful planning for her future, should she happen to outlive him, her intermittent generosity toward her employee had been overly casual.

Retrieving her checkbook from the tidy interior of her handbag, Mrs. Westfield propped herself against the door frame and wrote a generous check. Handing it over to Janette, she said, "Let me know how you're getting along. Maybe we can work something out in the future. After all, we have been such good friends."

Janette accepted the check, looked at it and grunted. There was no vestige of the woman whose company had been such a delight over the long years. "Mrs. Westfield," she said, "you were a decent person to work for but I don't know how somebody like you and somebody like me could ever be "friends."

She said "friends" as if such a thought had never occurred to her in all the twenty years of association between the two women.

Mrs. Westfield went home and lay down with cold compresses on her head. Later, she would make calls to cancel the meeting of the travel club. Even later, she would talk to someone, the pastor of her church or her physician, someone who could help her make sense of the pain she felt at what she perceived as Janette's spitefulness.

There were certain things she knew she could never do. Certainly, she could never compromise her standards of how a home should be run. Whatever she ultimately ended up by doing, she would have to manage on her own for some time, perhaps entertaining less and possibly adjusting her housekeeping program.

She wondered whether it would be reasonable to forego ironed sheets and dish towels but that was rather drastic and would be a decision she would make later.

SPECIAL DELIVERY

THERE WAS A DOWNRIGHT DEARTH of professional people in Millwell. The town seemed to have a hostile streak that disallowed the affection that other places held for an old doctor, a country lawyer, a long-time cleric. These professions were frequently represented along Main Street but the people who performed them came and then went away fairly quickly.

Exceptions were two men who, when together, formed a sort of shadow chorus about what was going on within town limits. Doc Pinster, a dentist whose office and dingy living quarters were up over the bank, and Manny Streeter, who ran the post office and lived in a tidy apartment upstairs in that building, had been local citizens for years. They had not been born in the town and did not, in the long run, become aged and die there—but in the interim years they took a silent interest. Manny, in particular—perhaps because the local post office was the hub of much that went on in Millwell—felt a certain responsibility for the town's wellbeing.

Despite seeing it all, they never made waves. Bachelors, they were soft-bodied, quiet-spoken people who rarely, if ever, disclosed their past lives, their interests or their personal problems. World War II was going on during some of their sojourn in Millwell but neither of them was personally involved since they were a little too old and a little too flabby.

From his dental chair perch above the bank, Doc Pinster recognized most of the people who worked and shopped on Main Street and those who came to town on Saturdays to trade their eggs and listen to the evening band concert. Some of them came to him to have their teeth fixed and many more came to have theirs yanked out to make way for dentures. While business wasn't bad, some people never got around to paying him and he didn't send out bills.

About every other weekend, Doc picked up Shirley Spence and they went to one of the nearby county seat towns to do some grocery shopping, eat dinner and go to a show. Afterward, Doc would drop Shirley off at her house and go back to his rooms behind the dental office.

Shirley ran the switchboard at Millwell's telephone office. "Number please," she said, over and over, as the local people called each other to exchange gossip or conduct whatever business defined their lives. Sometimes she was asked to set up a long distance call but long distance calls were expensive so infrequently done. Boys in the service called home sometimes, but not often, relying instead on letters. Their mothers and grandmothers then responded with their own letters.

Shirley was bound by the rules of Bell Central to keep everything she heard over the line to herself and was good about that—although Doc sometimes maneuvered her into sharing an occasional tidbit with him. At those times, Shirley would smile a thin smile and pass a hand over her nicely permed hair, pushing it back to tidy repose over her ears.

"You keep that quiet," she would caution Doc. "I just think somebody besides me ought to know. You wouldn't believe the things that go on in Millwell!"

The United States Postal Service was as firm as Bell Central about its employees. Manny Streeter took all the rules to heart and was sort of an over-achiever when it came to minding his own business. When the mail pouches came in and he distributed their contents, he was circumspect about not reading all of the postcards or making many conjectures about who was writing to whom. There were occasions when he took extra interest but he never allowed himself to engage in spoken speculation.

As he sat on his high stool at the post office counter, he actually had little need for guesswork. People came and went as they checked their mail, bought stamps and sent packages. A certain number of them, mostly older women, stopped to talk. Often lonely, they were inclined to tell Manny everything they knew about local activity and some of them tried very hard to worm information out of him.

"I guess the Schultz girl's wedding is going to be big doings," a woman would say, assuming that the invitations would have had to go out from the post office

"The Schultz's have a lot of relatives," he might answer, knowing full well how many invitations had been sent and to whom and taking care to never divulge that knowledge.

He was the soul of discretion in all respects. If, as often happened, someone who stood in front of his postal window talked a lot about herself, her worrisome children, her alcoholic husband, he listened kindly and once in a while offered mild advice, softening it with, "Well, I've heard...." However, he never repeated the conversation to anyone else.

When he went upstairs to his apartment after the day ended, few local events stayed on his mind. After heating up a can of stew or soup, he ate while listening to classical music on the radio. Later, he did cross word puzzles or perused his collection of National Geographic magazines. Never, ever did he telephone anyone, even an aunt whose health worried him.

"Shirley Spence or one of her part-timers will be listening," he said to himself. While few of his phone calls would have provided the town with anything interesting about his extra-Millwell life, the surer route to privacy was to keep himself to himself. An occasional exception was when he and Doc Pinster talked. He might tell Doc that he was thinking of going to Yellowstone Park when he had some time off, or maybe taking the train to Washington, D. C. so he could spend a few days at the Smithsonian. When it came to Manny, Doc was good about keeping his mouth shut, and a useful conversation could be had.

In his own way, Doc was a student of human behavior and made up small theories for his own amusement. The view from his dental chair took in a good part of Millwell's main drag. That included who visited the pool hall, the implement dealership, the meat storage locker, the drug store. His educated guesses included who was out of a job, which farmers were prosperous, what housewife was expecting company and which of the town's servicemen was home on furlough.

The clearest but least interesting view from Doc's window was the loafers' bench and its occupants who sat in front of the grocery store in the mornings and in front of the pool hall in the afternoons. It always held the same retired men, who went home for dinner at noon and came back an hour or two later to take up their observation posts. Indeed, their conversations were limited to the most basic of local news and the pedigree of the people who passed by. That was obvious from their low-key body language. No degree of excitement was ever discerned. They had all been fitted with dentures long ago so Doc rarely had cause to converse with any of them directly. "Just waitin' for the undertaker," somebody once said to Doc, nodding in the direction of the idlers. Doc told that to Manny, thinking the comment pretty funny, and with typical sweet gravity, Manny said, "They could be doing worse."

Doc often noted small out-of-the-ordinary changes in the loafers and filed them in the back of his brain. A man's steady absence was likely a sign that an illness or death had occurred. Recurrent and worsening slovenliness might indicate the demise of a spouse.

Occasionally, a bench that was empty due to a surfeit of sun on its side of the street would come to be occupied by a person of unknown identity. Doc enjoyed those times and would guess to himself who the individual was and what they were doing in Millwell. Most often, it was somebody waiting for a pre-arranged ride; the waited-for car or truck would eventually round the corner by the Shell station and its driver would stop to pick up the waiting stranger.

Doc realized after one or two such occurrences that the same run-down truck often showed up and that it belonged to Banty Long. Banty was so called because he was short and squat and presented himself as if he was very important. "Banty" was a nickname that, in Millwell parlance, stood for "bantum rooster." He'd picked it up in high school and was used to it, even though Wilbur was his given name.

Banty was giving up his teeth, one by one, to Doc, never presenting himself at the dental office until he was suffering from a monumental tooth ache.

"Why don't you just let me pull 'em all?" Doc would ask. "Then you can go ahead and get a dental plate. You'll be able to eat better and won't have to go through the misery of one toothache after another."

"I ain't rollin' in money," Banty would answer Doc, but it was known that he lived alone, put in a good sized vegetable garden every spring and sold the produce to local grocery stores, and also generated a small amount of cash by farming on shares. He could have afforded false teeth, Doc knew, or he wouldn't have asked.

Watching Banty roll up one day to pick up the waiting stranger on the loafers' bench, Doc realized something interesting—the strangers all looked quite similar. Youngish men, skinny, they had an aura of being down on their luck. Since they were of an age to be drafted, most had probably been rejected as 4F. Some appeared relatively clean, others pretty begrimed; not one was recognizable as a local.

"I wonder where Banty finds his hired help," Doc said to Manny.

One Saturday he said that to Shirley, too, as they made their way to the A & P in Denison. Shirley's hazel eyes opened wide. Without prompting, she volunteered a wonder of her own.

"He's such a disagreeable person," she said, "that I'm always surprised when guys call him up and want to come work for him."

"Millwell guys?" asked Doc.

"Likely not. Millwell people wouldn't have to call him long distance."

Doc's hearing sharpened. "Who'd call him long distance?"

Shirley laughed. "People who don't live here! Seems like the calls always come from Omaha or Council Bluffs or somewhere down there. They must not stay very long after they're hired because a month or two later here comes another call from some gas station in no-man's land. Banty must tack up 'help wanted' notes all over the place."

After seeing Banty pick up yet another vagrant type from the north side loafer's bench, Doc reported it to Manny almost immediately. "If he's hiring these guys to work for him, they must not find the job satisfactory. They're moving on sooner and sooner, for some reason."

Manny wasn't used to hearing concern in Doc's voice so he made a mental note to sharpen his own eyes and ears. However, nobody who came into the post office mentioned Banty Long in any way.

Just as he was losing interest, one rainy day here came the man himself into the lobby. Manny straightened up, expecting a conversational exchange or two and maybe a roundabout answer to the mystery.

"Two stamps," Banty said, holding out a dime.

"Get rained out of the field?" Manny politely asked.

No answer.

Manny pushed the stamps toward Banty, surprised and offended at the snub. "Here you go," he said.

"Yeah, Streeter," Banty said, scooping up the stamps and his pennies of change, then stomping out the door, almost bumping into Mrs. August Grassley who was old and tiny, with a back almost folded double from her spinal problems. Manny was offended for Mrs. Grassley's sake and equally as offended for himself. He hadn't been addressed in such a dismissive tone—and by just his last name—since long ago school days and he associated it with memories of bullying.

"Streeter!" he said to himself, as shamed recollections of weeping in schoolyard corners flooded his mind.

When Doc told him, only days later, that Banty had picked up yet another vagrant type from the loafers' bench, Manny was pretty much over his anger but had an unfamiliar yen for revenge. Something should be done, he thought, to prevent Banty from taking advantage of poor young guys who just wanted to have a job. Whatever he was doing, whether refusing to pay them for work done, or firing them at the first ineptitude, he should be stopped.

Stopping Banty became something of an obsession for Manny. With the same dedication he usually applied to his cross word puzzles, he entertained ideas of varying impracticality. Visions of confronting Banty interfered with pleasanter visions rising from the Saturday afternoon opera broadcast. As he shaved, combed his sparse hair over a widening bald spot, and filed his finger nails, Manny contemplated possibilities. It came to him that somebody should go out to Banty's farm and see what was going on.

Dismissing thoughts of Millwell's mayor and the town marshal as candidates for snooping, he said to himself, "I guess it would have to be me!" Once he made that discovery, he lay awake for two nights thinking up schemes. What excuse could a postmaster find for making an uninvited visit?

Banty's mail, such as he had, was delivered by the rural mail carrier and that individual, Glen Roberson, was a busy family man who wanted to finish his routes as quickly as possible. He would, Manny thought, be the wrong person to send on such an exploration. Manny thought Glen made entirely too much money for what he did, but knew Glen thought the same of him and they didn't talk much. Certainly, no discussion of Banty's incessant hiring of farm help had ever taken place.

With something like terror, Manny drew upon his own personal ingenuity. "Well," he said, addressing his image in his bathroom mirror, "it looks like Banty needs to get a special delivery letter."

But nobody was ever going to send a special delivery letter to Banty, Manny thought. That meant he was going to have to manufacture one and that was dabbling in something that the United States Postal Department would regard very severely. If he did this thing, nobody could know, ever, and that included Doc.

Familiar with the intrusions that could be exerted by female relatives, Manny first wondered if the vagrants who went to work on the Banty Long farm didn't have family that cared. A mother? he thought, narrowing down his speculations. Wouldn't one of the mothers be curious about the wellbeing of her drifter son?

An inquiring letter would have to be written by Manny but Manny's personal stationery wouldn't do. Light blue, unlined, with a nice little monogram that entwined an "M" and an "S" at the top, it gave him immense pleasure when he had an excuse to use it. It was pleasantly masculine, he thought, and offered unspoken class to his persona. It would be entirely inappropriate for a searching mother with an undoubtedly limited life.

Making a little trip across the street from the post office to the Millwell drug store, Manny chose a ruled tablet of pulp paper and minimal price. Its cover image of Rita Hayworth—which he preferred to one of the Andrews Sisters—spoke eloquently of the buyers it targeted but the drug store clerk seemed to find it a natural item for just about anybody to buy. Manny diminished its importance further by adding a box of cough drops, a couple of number two pencils, and a pack of plain envelopes.

That night he lay awake thinking what to write and what names to use. The phantom mother of a phantom vagrant should have a name that was pretty common but maybe a little hard to remember.

"Plenty of syllables," he said to himself.

"Theresa Welterstrauss" was his eventual and creative choice. "Theresa" was a reasonably ordinary name but not much used locally. "Welterstrauss" had an echo of mid-America ethnicity while not a name in Millwell's phone book.

"Six syllables with some hard consonants," Manny mused.

After work the next day, Manny got out the Rita Hayworth tablet and set to work concocting a handwriting that bore no resemblance to his own meticulous script. "Dear Mr. Long," began the letter. "I am looking to here about my son, Arthur. About two months ago I had a postal card from him that said he was going to work for you in Millwell. I'm not here from him since then. If he is at your place, will you ask him to write to me? If he left alredy, I will like to no that. Thank you. Mrs. Theresa Welterstrauss."

Manny reviewed his work with a sense of accomplishment. Clever, he thought, to spell "hear" as "here," misspell a word or two, and include the self-applied title of "Mrs." He'd seen enough local postcards to know that was norm for some folks.

Addressing one of the newly purchased envelopes to "Mr. Wilbur Long, RR 2, Millwell, Iowa," he again wrote "Mrs. Theresa Welterstrauss," this time as a return address. Obviously, the fictional Mrs. Welterstrauss would have to live somewhere so, after a fair amount of thought, Manny added "276 Jones St., Sioux City, Iowa" to the return. Whether or not there actually was a 276 Jones Street was immaterial.

Sioux City wasn't exactly next door to Millwell but it was within 60 or so miles. It would have mailboxes on some street corners and a letter could be posted in one of them, then sent on to its designated recipient for a likely next-day postal delivery to the addressee.

A light in the post office after closing time might bring an investigation from Millwell's night watchman so Manny waited until the next morning to buy a special delivery stamp from himself. Ten cents for that and another few cents for a regular stamp did the trick. What he had to do next was distasteful but there was no help for it. As soon as the post office was locked for the day, he got in the tidy tan Chevrolet Special Deluxe which he had purchased just before automobile manufacture ceased and all factories dedicated to the war effort. It had a pretty full tank of gasoline, enough to get him to Sioux City, and he set forth on his Machiavellian trip.

Darkness fell quite late that time of summer but, even so, Manny wasted no time driving back home after a handy mailbox on the corner of an older Sioux City neighborhood swallowed the letter. He felt no inclination to linger in the downtown for a bite to eat; Sioux City offended his aesthetic tastes. The whole city was on the shabby side, he thought, and then there was that unpleasant aura from the stockyards when the wind was blowing. There had been talk for years about something called "urban renewal" but no signs it was happening. "Hard telling," Manny said, addressing the Chevy's windshield, "what kind of people live here. I picked the right place, all right."

Whoever the citizens of Sioux City were, they had efficient postal workers. Mrs. Theresa Welterstrauss's letter arrived in Millwell a day and a half later and its special delivery stamp dictated the next move. It must be taken to its addressee and by a proper postal worker. First, however, Manny took care to let Glen Roberson, the rural mail carrier, know such a letter existed—but only after Glen had finished his day's deliveries and was ready to go home.

"I'll take it out there," he told Glen. "I've been meaning to get out in the country for a look at how the corn is doing."

While the progress—or lack of it—of the corn crop was of scant interest to Manny, it would, he thought, make for a few nice little discussions with tomorrow's post office patrons. By the time he got to Banty Long's turn-off lane, with glances to the fields right and left of the road, he had already justified to himself the validity of the drive. Somehow, he felt particularly competent, a regular citizen of Millwell with something useful to offer and he sat taller in his seat.

The lane, however, was a disaster. A car like Manny's should never be driven on its miserably deep ruts, and probably never was because the rural mail carrier only had to pause beside the mail box on the gravel road. A pickup, and not a very good one at that, would be the vehicle of choice for the lane.

With his eyes already attuned to the progress of corn, Manny saw that Banty's crop was hardly worth observing. The edges of the half-hearted fields and the lane itself were, instead, dumping spots for a mixture of decrepit farm machinery. In his effort to squeeze past a worn out hay wagon that was minus a hitch, Manny hit a rut that sent him jouncing straight up in the air; he came down feeling deprived of the sense of well being with which he had entered the lane.

"Be lucky if I get out of here without damaging the car," he said to himself. He then shrank further, anticipating his coming encounter with Banty Long. The house lay just ahead, a shabby two-story dwelling that had likely seen better days before the depression of the '30s. It had a dangerously leaning porch that was cluttered with battered pails and dirty shovels.

Taking a moment, ostensibly to locate the special delivery letter from the car's passenger side, but actually to get a good look at the vegetable garden that sprawled over a very large piece of land where a lawn and grazing acreage might once have been, Manny was startled to see a kind of apparition headed toward him.

"Must be one of those vagrants that Doc talks about," he thought. The word "vagrant" came easily to mind because the apparition-like being was a young and emaciated-looking man who looked anxiously toward Manny and was obviously trying to cover the ground between them as fast as possible. His progress was limited, however, because it looked as if one of his legs was attached to something that held him back.

No time to speculate. The house door opened as if kicked and a furious Banty stormed out onto the porch, peered to identify the car and driver that had violated his privacy, and yelled, "Streeter! What the fuck you want? And you, you son of a bitch, get back to your hoeing!"—the last addressed to the ragged young man in the garden.

Manny had not been as terrified in all his adult years and he took in the whole scene—the quivering person who was trying to get to him, the raging Banty Long, the special delivery letter in his hand, as if they were all at the end of a nightmare tunnel. Nevertheless, he consciously straightened his back, then slid out of the car and approached Banty—very slowly and deliberately to be sure—and held out the letter.

"You got a special delivery letter," he said, "and it's the law that I have to bring it to you. It's not my choice; blame Uncle Sam."

Whether startled by the reference to Uncle Sam or stunned by a sudden sense of caution, Banty did an unlikely thing. He opened his mouth wide in an ingratiating smile that displayed a few yellow stumps and said, "Much obliged, Streeter. Be careful of them machinery ruts when you drive out."

When he was safely home and had time to reflect, Manny decided it was of no use to call up the town watchmen or the county sheriff to report what he'd seen. Both would try to placate him—the Millwell night watchmen, the town's only law officer, because he would think it was none of his business and the sheriff because he couldn't go running all over the county investigating mere possibilities.

"Another Theresa Welterstrauss letter coming up," Manny said to himself and after scraping his half-eaten dinner into the garbage pail, he got out the Rita Hayworth tablet and one of the pencils and wrote: "Dear Sheriff, I do not no what to do. My boy Arthur Welterstrauss told me he was going to work for Mr. Wilbur Long in Millwell. I have not here from him since so I asked my brother and his son to go out to see Wilbur Long and find out if my boy is still at his place. They went out there but nobody was home so they looked around and saw a big crop of pot plants in the far end of the yard. No way those plants can be mixed up with anything else!!!

I am asking will you investigate and see if you can see my missing son?"

Manny affixed a special delivery stamp to the letter and headed for Sioux City as soon as he could get away from the post office. He had pulled the best trick he knew by fingering Banty Long as a pot raiser. The county sheriff might ignore hints of abuse to farm workers but there was no way he would fail to go after somebody breaking the law by raising marijuana.

Having done all that he knew to do, Manny went back to sitting on the stool behind the post office window and hoped he'd at least hear rumors if anything came of his letter.

He didn't have to wait for very long. It was all over town before three days had gone by. Shirley Spence heard things on the phone lines that gave her nightmares the rest of her life. The sheriff and his deputy had gone out to Banty Long's farm with a search warrant and Banty hadn't wanted to let them in the house. No wonder. There were piles of old pants and scuffed suitcases scattered all around in the dark, filthy upstairs rooms. The stuff had to have belonged to other guys because the clothes sure wouldn't have fit Banty.

Besides, there was incriminating evidence outdoors. While the sheriff didn't find any marijuana plants, lo and behold they did find at least twenty shallow graves with naked corpses. None of the bodies could be identified because they were too decomposed and hacked up. On top of that, there was no way to use dental records because all the victims' teeth had been knocked out. There was evidence, said some of those who had insider information, of torture and perverse sexual activity.

Others suggested that cannibalism had been involved. "Not likely," Doc said to Manny when they next talked. "That s.o.b. couldn't have eaten a plate of boiled cabbage, the shape his teeth were in!"

Banty Long couldn't be asked because he hanged himself in the county jail on the very first night he was locked up.

In all his life, Manny never told anyone about the special delivery stamps and all the rest of it, including his trips to Sioux City mailboxes. Once in a while, when he needed a little self-confidence, he did say to himself, " I faced down a murderer!"

But he also never forgot the terrified look on the face of the young man who had struggled across the field to reach him when he drove his tan Chevy into Banty Long's farmyard.

SHE

SHE WAS CARMEN and she had never heard of Carmen. She was eleven and she was nothing. She stood in the half-dark garage with her back against the big door and her arms flung out wide, wide and beautiful against the peeling wood. Her breath came in lovely, deliberate gasps and she tossed long phantom hair until the crimson roses loosened, falling to hard-packed dirt.

Against the walls, behind the hazardous hooks and nails, beyond the paint-splattered ladders and rusty hoes and hand-worn rakes with tired dry grass between the tines, were the crowds that cheered, that laughed, that sang, that adored. A maple tree outside the small, lone window trembled and shadows sifted through a beam of dust as she spit between her teeth.

"I will be beautiful and treacherous," she panted, and before her the misty men knelt and wept. There she stood, unmoving, the knife quivering in her heart, her lovely, swelling breast a sheltering sentinel.

"I am above them all, and unconquerable and how they love me!"

She fell to the earth and a winged ant that might have been a soul and was a termite took its leave and sank into one of the cracks in the foundation.

She rose from the dead and went out into the world. (You were not supposed to play in the garage. The garage was only for the speckled ladders and for the old Ford panel truck that coughed into it at six every evening.)

She walked with studied grace in the old white satin formal that had been sent from the cousins in the East. It was to have been made over into something for her but the mother had seen that it was not suitable and had given it into her tense, craving hands. It now hung in unfulfilled folds, disreputable and streaked with a line of blood—blood not from her treacherous, flaming heart but from the mangled foot of the bird she had found caught in the barbed wire of Waterman's cornfield.

Tenderly, she cradled it and wondered what to do to help it. She

31

made it a bed in a little box, lining the box with grass and the heads of marigolds, thinking if it died she would make a funeral and bury it in one of the rich mounds of dirt cast up in Noah's acre by the gophers.

Carrying the box, the evening dress caught up daintily in a long, white phantom hand, she walked across the back yard, picking her way around the damp spots where they dumped the slops. The bird in the box was still and oblivious to the engulfing waves of maternalism. He was the child, the lover, dying. She would visit his grave each day at dusk and lay upon it a sheaf of newly opened four-o'-clocks and they would see her in her flowing robes with all that was best of dark and light meeting in her aspect and her eyes.

She walked around the outside of the house and set the box down on the front porch. The porch was a warp, a sag, an annex of gray unpaintedness with illusions of grandeur. It might have been built to satisfy a long-ago carpenter who wanted to add something fancy to the succession of boxcar rooms that was the house. It ran the width of the house, high above the ground, and was reached by crumbling cement steps, its roof upheld by two dilapidated columns.

At the side of the steps were high risers and on one of these she now stood. She stretched out her arms in gracious benediction and she was Athena, goddess of wisdom, guarding her temple. Below her knelt the supplicating throng, one man nearer than the others. She bent down and touched his shoulder and said, "Go, and sin no more," and the man bowed his head in reverence.

Delivered of oracles, she picked up the box with bird and grass and went out to Noah's, a plot of ground always so called by the father because it divided the family's ground. Because it belonged to Mr. Noah, it could not be put into vegetable garden like the rest. Noah's was given over to matted grass and gopher hills and it was the moor where the rings of fairies danced in the moonlight. She was Tatiana, queen of the fairies, and stalked the grassy flats with the key from a sardine can, ready to unlock the secret doors in the trees. Mischievous, gay, more loved than anyone, she glided toward the raspberry bushes that grew just at the edge of the moor.

Then the back screen door slammed and the mother came out onto the back stoop, carrying a bucket of scrub water. She was tired, dirty, snappy and angry. She worked all day, every day, with reddened hands and she had a daughter who never thought to do the things a girl of eleven could do to help out. The mother screamed a tired, angry scream before returning to the kitchen, "If you can stop your play-baby stuff long enough, you can help with supper!"

She picked up the box with the nearly dead bird and threw the key into it. Eyes down with guilty dread, she left Noah's. On the way to the house she stopped in back of the garage and lifted the lid of the old wash boiler that served as a garbage can. She threw the box on top of the cans of coagulated paint and the stinking feathers from Sunday's chicken dinner, closed the lid and walked to the house.

Through the west window, shafts of weak summer sunlight fell across the worn linoleum, the patched kitchen walls and the scarred table where Carmen and Athena, Tatiana and she sat slicing the potatoes for frying.

Dene Hellman

CANDIDATE MATERIAL

IF NEWCOMERS TO Center Plaines were lucky, they were referred to Red Leonard's automobile maintenance shop. "You can't beat it," they were told. "Those folks are knowledgeable, they're honest, and they're quick." Nobody said they were cheap. Actually, Red charged more than a lot of other places for routine maintenance jobs. But maybe his customers saved quite a bit of money in the long run because Red's mechanics never came into the waiting room to tell the owner of the car they were working on that she needed a new oil pan or brake lining or muffler. Except, of course, in those cases where such an item actually was needed—and then it was Red who did the explaining.

He was pleased about the little stories that were circulated about his honesty and the skill exhibited by his employees and, childishly, sometimes reviewed them as he drifted off to sleep at night.

"My battery kept running down," said one lady, who had no pretensions to knowing anything about cars, "and I was all set to spend some money on the electrical system. I would have believed anything I was told. When I took the car to Red, his mechanic started laughing after a three minute examination. Red explained that my dome light was on all the time and that was making the battery run down, so have a good day and no charge!"

Simple stories but they added up.

Red didn't put down the people who learned auto mechanics from courses they'd taken at the county's technical college. In fact, he was often invited over there to talk to the classes about his philosophy of car repair. However, his people—all men, although not for chauvinistic reasons—were guys who had gathered around an automobile, any automobile available for looking, since they were 12 years old: guys who talked cars, dreamed cars and esteemed all cars worthy of attention, no matter how old or new the vehicle.

This respect was evident when one looked at the lot in front of Red's garage. In addition to many shiny late model cars, there was Eunice Plover's 15 year old Lexus, Nan Somer's 1999 Honda CRV, and Jack Welles's 2003 Ford Taurus, all purchased new once upon a time and continuing in the best of shape.

"You can drive this clear out to the East Coast without a speck of trouble," Red liked to say to them, nodding his head with its shock of auburn hair when he handed back their keys and accepted their money. These customers had enough pride to bring their aging vehicles in at decent intervals for proper maintenance, and Red had enough pride to encourage them to continue driving with confidence.

Compared to the repair departments of new car dealerships, Red Leonard's garage was cosmetically challenged, the better to encourage a "business only" atmosphere. No piped in music, no magazines less than five years old, no comfy chairs. The coffee pot was always on but the brew was bitter. The television was overhead and angled more for the benefit of Red when he was passing through than it was for waiting customers. The only thing that provided any aesthetic pleasure was Red's wife, Mary Susan, when she came out of her little bookkeeping room to help out with customers who needed a bit of credit or a ride home because their vehicle was going to have to stay overnight. Mary Susan may have been close to fifty years of age but she was tall, slim, sweet of face and wore pretty sweaters with well-fitting jeans. Red knew his wife was a terrific asset to the business, even though she didn't know a muffler from a spare tire, and he was proud of her. Plus, Mary Susan had an uncanny ability to put names with faces. Walking through the waiting room, she'd call out a greeting to old Mr. Bundy who was waiting for his car's annual inspection to be finished or Miss Wilson, who had brought her 1993 Buick for Red's magic touch every few months since buying it secondhand in 1995. If Mary Susan saw a person once, she knew that person forever after as well as the car owned by that individual.

Center Plaines was the state capital, one of a mere handful of large towns in a state full of people who earned their livelihoods at work that required large tracts of land. However, due to the shop's location, some of Red's customers were involved in government, either as permanent fixtures with special skills or as people who had been voted into office— even as other customers were voted out of office and went back home to their small towns or ranches.

Red was fairly apolitical and casual about most issues. Three decades before, he had acquired a degree at the state university, a degree that had never been of the slightest use to him. He'd been much more likely to work on a fellow classmate's ailing vehicle than to read up on European history or American literature and possibly the only reason he'd squeaked through to a diploma was because he had racked up several successes with an aging Mercedes owned by the Dean of Men. He never quite recovered from his surprise that Mary Susan had agreed to marry him. She always laughed when he told her that and insisted that she had thought it amazing, when she met him, that a guy that sexy could also be so open, honest and cheerful.

So, there it was. He was a nice guy who knew the way to a lot of hearts was through intimacy with a person's car's cooling system. Doing well in his own business, he often contributed equal amounts to both parties in an election. Since it wasn't greatly inconvenient, Red also sat on a few State committees that focused on highway maintenance and the upkeep of state landmarks. It kept him on a first-name basis with lots of people, kept the cash register humming as new acquaintances brought in their autos, and gave his beloved Mary Susan something to chatter about over late dinners at their bistro of choice.

When a party bigwig came into Red's garage one mid-term and told him that his state and his country needed him, Red's first reaction was to wonder if there was something wrong with the automobile fleet in use by the party stalwarts.

"Nah," said Bob Anderson, who was a Democrat and a permanent fixture in the state government, due to his communications expertise. "What we need is for you to run for United States Senator. That asshole that's represented us for the last 18 years finally went too far with his booze and skirt chasing and made a drunken grab at the Vice President's niece. He's been invited to resign by a bunch of important people and has decided to take them up on it."

"Why me?" asked Red.

"You're honest, you're natural, people like you, you have a terrific family and you'd look great on television," was Bob Anderson's terse reply.

"Can you believe that guy?" Red said to Mary Susan over dinner that evening. "He said I'm better known than a lot of Party regulars and they have to run somebody known for being ethical to make up for the hush-hush about the guy we've sent to Washington for three terms. I told him I'd think it over and talk to you, but that was just a polite way of letting him down easy."

Mary Susan looked thoughtful and said something totally unexpected. "If you want my opinion, you should do it," she said.

Red almost choked on his grilled salmon. "WHAT?" he said, loudly enough to turn heads at nearby tables. "Why would I want to do that?"

"Because," Mary Susan said, "there are a lot of things that need attention paid. Education for one. The infrastructure for another. It's been years since we sent anybody to Congress who cared a hoot about anything beyond tax exemptions or the price of beef."

"What about the business?" asked Red, even though what Mary Susan said gave him a nice little mental picture of himself with a gavel in hand, ordering one or another of those Senate nincompoops to shut up and sit down.

"Just as we do now, whenever we're away from the garage," said Mary Susan. "Call in your dad. He'll be thrilled to take over for you on a temporary basis. After all, you learned about cars from him and he's always telling you what you should and shouldn't do. He gets bored in that Sun City resort he and your step mother live in and lives for the times you need him."

"How can you call it 'temporary?'" asked Red. "Do you realize that running for an office like Senator takes the better part of a year—and then another six years after you're elected?"

"Ha!" said Mary Susan. "When people run for office they get to say things out loud that need saying. As for being elected, can you tell me the last time this state elected a Democrat?"

"You got a point," said Red.

The next day he told Bob Anderson that he'd do it, by golly, but was going to need a lot of help to avoid mistakes.

"Don't worry about that," said Bob. "I'm the communications expert. I write speeches; I oversee television ads; I set up schedules and decide what needs to be said and where to say it."

Before they could catch their breaths, Red and Mary Susan were off on a six-month merry-go-round that took them into every corner of the state and on a few junkets to Washington, D.C. to meet with important people. When Red was invited to make a speech at some event, Bob wrote him one that sounded authentic and Red was sufficiently astute to handle himself with composure during any question and answer period that ensued. It didn't seem a lot different to him from explaining to a budget-strained teacher why she needed to change the timing belt in her aging car. The need was there; the facts were there; it was a matter of understanding the necessity to get it done.

Mary Susan was terrific. Often, she was scheduled to address some woman's gathering in a private home or at one of the events that attracted a good-sized female crowd. She had easily picked up the program the party was promoting and had plenty of ideas of her own to round out the rest. The women adored her, some of the older ones recollecting for one another how, way back, Rosalynn Carter had helped Jimmy with his peanut business before he went into politics and then had moved right on over to the campaign trail.

Whenever Mary Susan and Red were some place where there were previously met people, it was Mary Susan who would call out, "Ms. Roberts! How great to see you again! We really need your good help. And is this your husband?"

Contributions rolled in, a lot of them from rural women.

Eventually, much as he enjoyed the socializing and exchange of ideas, Red got scared. And not for the usual reasons for a candidate to get cold chills. It was becoming obvious that people liked him enough to put him in danger of *getting elected*.

Even his Republican opponents were nice to him. Some of them had known him for years, valued his opinions about their vehicles, and thanked him for his contributions to their own campaigns. They just couldn't bring themselves to say negative things about him and had to stick to issues. What a quandary.

In October, a month before election day, the League of Women Voters in Center Point announced an upcoming debate, all candidates expected. The Leaguers were thought to be a little skewed toward the liberal side of things but that didn't stop them from asking a fierce and unbiased newscaster—George Winslow—to be the moderator of the verbal contest between Red and his Republican opponent, Ralph Ringgold.

In preparation for the event, Bob Anderson and other party stalwarts undertook to rehearse Red. Mock symposiums were set up, likely questions were asked, answers were timed and critiqued. But Red was not particularly cooperative, and Mary Susan came down hard on him for that. "Quit dragging your feet," she said. You've done so well just by being the great person you are, all the newspapers and periodicals are predicting an astounding win for you."

Flattering as all of that was, Red became unusually pensive during the countdown days until the debate. He scrupulously attended all of the debate rehearsals and answered all of the practice questions politely and reasonably but his lack of humor and spirit worried his handlers.

"If I didn't know better," Bob Anderson said to the others, "I'd think he's either coming down with stomach trouble or his best friend just disowned him."

"Not to worry," said the other state Democrats who were helping with debate preparation. "Red is probably just getting stage fright. He'll be his old self again as soon as he sees the debate audience and all those cameras."

Mary Susan and the others were considerably cheered when, on the day of the event, Red seemed to have regained his natural good-humor. He wasn't particularly conversational but was his customary affectionate self to Mary Susan and before he took himself to the waiting microphones and cameras he shook Bob Anderson's hand at great length and with vigor.

"Thank you for everything," he said, in extremely warm tones.

From behind the scenes, he watched Mary Susan work the room, shaking hands and, of course, flattering everyone by calling them by name. She was in her element.

A melancholy expression came and went on his face so quickly that it might not have happened at all. He and Ralph Ringgold took their places behind podiums; Ralph, a sober sort, made a gallant effort to nod and smile at people he knew. Red, whose presence was being well taken care of by Mary Susan and her never-ending grace, studied his note cards as if he was worried about recalling what debate points to make.

George Winslow, the debate moderator, slipped into place, shoulders back, spine upright. A steady presence on many of the

Sunday news review programs, he was a veteran at this debate thing. Ordinarily, he wouldn't have come out here to a plains state that was such an infrequent player in the hubbub of national politics. However, he'd been born and raised in this kind of place and was thus a bit sensitive about how neglected agricultural interests sometimes were. Besides, the University of this particular state had offered him an honorary degree at their next commencement if he showed up. "This debate is going to be a piece of cake," he said to himself. He'd ask his questions, work to clarify ambiguous answers and, overall, present himself in an astute manner that would, perchance, encourage a few sales when his next book came out.

Red won—or lost, depending upon one's attitude—the coin toss and so was first up to answer a question.

"Mr. Leonard," said George Winslow, "you have announced for a national office, that of United States senator. While that carries national responsibilities, if you win the election you will be a representative of this state. What do you plan to do to protect and enhance its agricultural well-being—specifically the raising and marketing of beef?"

"Well, Sir," said Red, who now looked so relaxed that he appeared to be lounging behind his lectern, "we do raise quite a few beef cows in this state and it is certainly in our best financial interest to market them efficiently. But I can't say as I am totally dedicated to that. There are a lot of health issues, you know. Myself, I eat quite a bit of fish."

The listeners in the auditorium and the people around the state who had tuned in to catch the debate gasped so audibly it was like a gust of wind arising from the plains.

George Winslow and the Republican senatorial candidate swallowed their own gasps but their faces took on a wide-eyed stare. They hadn't heard right, had they? Surely, it was some kind of a misbegotten joke and all would right itself in a moment or two.

"Mr. Ringgold?" said George Winslow, determined to lend no encouragement to frivolity.

Ralph Ringgold looked about one inhalation short of passing out at his opponent's answer but put together something of the response the voters expected. Not being overly quick when it came to adlibs, he went on for way too long about how he and his family ate a lot of beef and then his voice trailed off and his time was up.

Back to Red.

"Mr. Leonard," said George Winslow, a hint of nervousness in his voice, "one of the subjects that you frequently addressed in your campaign is the hazardous condition of our infrastructure, bridges in particular. I don't think many folks will deny the problem exists but the cost of fixing it is tremendous. How do you propose raising the money to pay for it?"

Red couldn't have looked more casual about fixing the problem. Coming around to the side of his podium, he first slouched against it, then leaned over and pulled up his socks.

"Well, Mr. Winslow," he said, "in my book, there really is an easy solution. Those companies all over the country who send their big rigs to carry their product around wherever they want had better step up to the plate. Their mammoth semi trucks, sometimes two of those monsters hitched together, cause the bridge and highway breakdowns so let 'em pay for fixing it. Keep them off the road entirely until they cough up a few extra billions."

"Mr. Ringgold?" said Mr. Winslow in something barely more than a whisper.

Ralph Ringgold's face was an open map of wonderment. He had been prepared by his folks to handle opposing opinions, but this was beyond expectations. He began with the usual platitudes that were always used when discussing omnipotent trucking firms and all their power over how and when livestock would be shipped—but then his voice trailed off.

George Winslow had recovered his poise. After all, he hadn't acquired his reputation as a communicator by being stumped by mere politicians. An attitude of comic querying was surely called for so he assumed an expression of semi-amusement.

"Mr. Leonard, you've thrown us a couple of curve balls this evening! Here's a question that deserves your serious consideration: many people have come over our borders during the past number of years and millions of refugees, worldwide, are struggling to find safety and solve the issues of shelter and food. What are your thoughts on the immigration situation?"

Red's face lost its casual look and he leaned forward to answer. "Mr. Winslow," he said, "I don't know what problem you're talking about. Do we need to call those folks by any name except 'people?'

41

Dene Hellman

My impression is that we got us some pretty nice folks settling into our state, just like my granddaddy was when he came from Poland and Mr. Ringgold's daddy was when he came down from Canada. Bring 'em on. If our state doesn't have enough space and food, what place does? Come to think of it, we can put 'em to work driving those trucks we need and fixing the bridges and roads to boot."

A hush. A hush emanating from George Winslow, from the audience, and from Ralph Ringgold. Mr. Winslow cleared his throat, drank some water, and asked for a rebuttal from Red's opponent.

Eventually, more platitudes were uttered and Mr. Winslow carried on. Many questions remained on his agenda and that was how many he intended getting through. It didn't matter what he asked, though. Red was sure to throw him off kilter. By now, the audience was laughing heartily at whatever was said and by whom. The writers for the evening talk shows would replicate the event for weeks.

Time for a last question and George Winslow asked it in a tone that was a fine mixture between relief and apprehension.

"Mr. Leonard," he said, "you have provided all of us with lots to think about. If you will, please tell us how you would vote if elected to the Senate from this state and called upon to decide if people can freely buy and carry firearms wherever they go."

"Well," said Red, "I wouldn't be for it. People can sure have their guns to use on their farms and ranches, but it's just asking for trouble to take those firearms any place else. You betcha, when trouble comes up, some nincompoop with a gun will handle it wrong nine times out of ten."

At last, it was over. Bob Anderson grabbed Red by the arm before he could even get off the podium. "Talk about some nincompoop not knowing their head from their ass!" he hissed. "What the hell did you think you were doing? We rehearsed answers to all those questions! The guy on the last bar stool in the seediest saloon in town could have done better!"

"Can't accuse me of platitudes. Now leggo my arm. You don't own me," said Red.

Stepping down, he went to his wife, gently put his arm around her shoulders, and they walked out into the October night.

42

"You deliberately threw it," said the quietly angry Mary Susan as they drove home.

"I'm sorry, Hon," said Red. "You really would have liked to go live in Washington for a while, wouldn't you?"

"Yes," said Mary Susan through gritted teeth. "This was our big chance to help accomplish important things!" Tears ran down her face.

The debate was a prime subject all over the country. Cartoonists drew according to their political beliefs but always featured a casual Red Leonard relaxing against a lectern, pulling up his socks. T-shirts with "I'M A RED LEONARD DEMOCRAT" accompanied by a cheerful face and a shock of auburn hair, were sold and worn everywhere in the country for at least six months. Standup comedians satirized the debate, sometimes trending toward Red, sometimes in sympathy with a startled George Winslow or a tongue-tied Ralph Ringgold.

Ringgold won the senatorial election, to nobody's surprise. Red might have stirred the feelings of a lot of registered and closeted Democrats, but the ultimate consensus was that he could be more of a maverick in Washington than was practical. Red was happy about that and called his opponent on election night with sincere good wishes. Subsequently, his business had a growth spurt and his customers, old and new, felt free to kid him about his celebrity status.

With earnest and frequent apologies, he tried making his debate performance up to Mary Susan with the long trip to Europe that she had always dreamed of. The smiles they got and the numbers of people who knew who they were and came up to shake their hands added to her pleasure. Depending upon the difficulty of the language spoken, she was quite successful in learning their names and, if she should ever chance to see them again, would be sure to recollect them.

Something over a year and a half later, Bob Anderson walked into the shop. Red greeted him cordially, with a handshake and a query as to Bob's current visit. Well aware that Bob had quit frequenting his automobile maintenance business after the debate, he asked, "What can we do for you?"

"Got another election coming up," said Bob in a noticeably cool voice. "Also, we have another senatorial race to run. Bill Schmidt has been in there for three terms and could probably win three more—but he's fighting lung cancer and is resigning. Maybe this time our Party will win the ring toss."

"Whoa!" said Red. "I'm not going to go for it, no matter how persuasive you are. You surely learned last time around that I'm not good candidate material."

Bob gave Red an unmistakably icy look.

"Didn't come in to talk to you," he said. "I'm a slow learner sometimes, but by now I know who the person is in your family who's a real scrapper and has the competence to win. Where's she at?"

"*Mary Susan*?" Red said.

"Mary Susan, indeed," Bob said, "and she has an appointment with destiny."

CONSUMER RESEARCH

MY POCKETS WERE EMPTY, if you know what I mean. There was enough in the bank most weeks to buy groceries and pay the rent but once in a while the utility companies had to wait a little bit to get all the money they said I owed them.

Cigarettes were something I'd left behind a long time ago. I've never hung out in bars but allowed myself a six pack of beer every week. That was about it for the luxuries although every once in a long while I would throw a steak on the grill or go see a movie when its actors were people I liked. Things I'd have liked to have and couldn't afford no way in hell: my own computer; a girlfriend; a mortgage; a car less than ten years old.

I had a job. It was a lousy job and only paid ten dollars an hour. There was a time when I worked in a situation that paid more than twice that so I'd enjoyed a few extras. Occasionally, I took a class in something that interested me, emailed friends and family when I felt like it, had the luxury of thinking some women weren't good enough for me, and so on. You get the picture. I was a regular person living like a regular person in a decent apartment. My car was new enough to be worth washing; I changed its oil myself but if I thought something was amiss I could take it over to the friendly neighborhood mechanic to fix.

Understand, I'm not complaining. The economy went bust and a lot of folks like me were caught in the undertow. Even so, some people stayed important, with a lot of money to spend while a bigger bunch of folks, like me, found out they weren't important at all, maybe never had been, and sure weren't going to amount to anything in the foreseeable future.

When television began boring me out of my skull—and that happened with greater frequency since I couldn't afford cable—I'd waste a little gas money and drive around town. Mostly, I looked at the cars other folks were driving and just for fun admire and/or criticize the vehicles that got my interest. I'd debate the merits of a Prius as if I was considering buying one. Saving gas is a good idea, considering how much it costs but then, about the time I decided a hybrid car would be a good choice, along would come a Hummer or a Mercedes or a BMW and my attention sharpened. I began to speculate how those vehicles must be pure driving pleasure and what they would do for me. They'd get me a classy woman, for sure! Once in a while I'd see an SUV with four or five of those cute little cartoons on the back—you know, two parent figures and two children and maybe a dog symbol, too. Those got to me especially hard. If I hadn't wasted my 30s tom-cating around from one woman to another, I'd probably have a family.

After a while, I started looking at houses and neighborhoods in that same consumer research way and feeling a little sheepish about it. About 35 years ago, my mother's idea of a good time on Sunday afternoon was having my dad drive us through upscale residential areas. It wasn't fun for me, but who cares what a five year old kid thinks? Mom commented on almost every house and yard she saw, like what color it should have been painted and whether or not the landscaping was appropriate. Without any visible jealousy, though; it was just for the pleasure of looking and pretending.

Dad probably detested those excursions but more from boredom than anything else. He made a good living as a foreman at the hosiery mill and our house was as good as the ones our friends and relatives had. He was just trying to give my mother a nice time. We all understood that a few people owned important companies and were out of our league, but that was okay.

Myself, I was always glad to get home so I could go out to our back yard and play on my swing set. Later, we'd make hot dogs on the grill and then kick back and watch the fireflies and listen to the summer noises coming from the city park swimming pool that was a few blocks over to the west.

Anyway, it maybe was some kind of nostalgia that was behind my interest when I began casing all the new housing that had gone up in places that were nothing but woods when I was a kid. The building styles were a lot more complicated than the ranch houses of my boyhood and it got to be similar to the time I spent looking at fancy cars. I'd pick out places where it would be nice to live, sometimes based on what I saw parked in the driveway or a grand landscaping layout.

A House for Her

Wondering was part of the fascination. What would people choose for furniture in a house that looked like something out of a television show about old time England? Or would that modernistic house across the street have a room where all this new electronic stuff would be used? Once in a while, when I was in the grocery store and had some time on my hands, I'd stop at the periodical rack and, just for fun, look at the different kinds of home decorating magazines. If somebody I knew came into the store, I'd quick put the magazine down and grab a *National Geographic* or *Time*. No use getting undeserved kidding for being thought girly.

And I didn't need the ideas. In my efficiency there wasn't more than a single bed, a little table, chairs for meals and a lounge chair for kicking back. Try rearranging a setup like that!

When I'd get tired of looking at fancy homes, I'd change focus from the mansions. There were plenty of streets located closer to town with big trees and some nice livable looking houses that were probably somebody's dream 40 years ago. Nothing very outstanding in today's world and too many of them had real estate signs out front, but I'd have given my shirt to have a couple of rooms in one of them. When I was growing up, widow ladies and other people who were trying to make ends meet would take in roomers. I would have made somebody a real good tenant! I could fix things for her and help with the lawn mowing.

When I got careless and cruised into the streets where I grew up, it was hurtful. The houses are now too shabby for anybody to actually choose to live there. The signs advertising a house for sale were in competition with the places that were obviously vacant. There was a broken down old Ford in front of the house where we once lived. It had a couple of tires missing and my folks would have been beside themselves over that eyesore if they still lived there but they'd long since moved to Greenville to take care of Mom's sister.

The place where I worked gave me a week off with pay in late June and there wasn't any question of being able to go anywhere, even to Greenville. Things I used to do, like camping out or going out to the lake to fish were not realistic because when I gave up my old apartment and moved into the efficiency, everything from my tent to fishing rods had to go for lack of storage space. I gave the stuff away and for about five minutes felt good that somebody could

47

Dene Hellman

use it. Then I'd take turns being mad or discouraged. There's a big permanent dent in the door of my efficiency where I just hauled off and gave it a kick when I moved in.

This cruising around looking at houses and cars resulted in something interesting during my week off from work. I'd gone to a library over on the prosperous side of town because they had a good-sized bunch of computers and not that many people competing for them. I was in the market for a better job and online is the way to go if you have that intent. Also, the librarians and volunteer assistants were usually nice women about my age and I enjoyed talking with them and asking their advice about this and that. I could daydream, couldn't I? I confided in a couple of them that I enjoyed looking at houses and they said I should think about becoming a realtor. The idea was sort of appealing but it would take money for the classes to attend, tests to take, and fees to pay. No use thinking about it.

Although great cars, fancy houses and smart, attractive women were definitely out of my reach, it belonged to my consumer research and there was no law against looking. When I left the library, I drove around some more and whoa! A fantastic looking house had something greater looking in the driveway. A Jaguar.

I slowed down to a barely decent speed, rubber necking all the way. Then I noticed a real nice looking lady working in a flower garden that stretched along the side of the house. She wasn't in especially fancy clothes, but she wasn't in grubs, either. She looked like she fit in and I was especially pleased when she looked up and gave me a nice smile and a nod. Not flirtatious, mind you, just nice, like the librarians.

I drove past her house later on that same week with the innocent intention of getting a better look at the Jag. Lo and behold, there was the same lady but, when I went to pass, I saw her keel over in the middle of the flowers. It looked like she was trying to deal with a heavy bag of something and it had gotten the best of her. She just laid there, either hurt or maybe knocked out. It didn't take me two minutes to pull up to the curb, jump out, and run over to see if she needed help. About that time, she sat up, rubbing her elbow, and looked at me tearing across the yard toward her.

"Are you okay?" I called out and she nodded while she tried to get to her feet.

"Thank you," she said. "I just tried to lift too much. This isn't something I ordinarily do so I don't have much gardening skill."

"Sit down," she added. "You are so sweet to try to help. If I'd really hurt myself, you would have been a godsend!"

I squatted down and sort of sat on my heels, trying to look debonair. "No problem," I said. "Just passing by on the way from the library and happened to look over this way."

"I'm Debbie," the lady said, sticking out her hand.

"Steve," I said, shaking her hand. Then I didn't know what else to say so I nodded toward the Jaguar. "How do you like it?" I asked, a stupid question if there ever was one.

"It's a good car," Debbie said, which was kind of an understatement.

"How do you like the Wright Place Library?" she asked. "They always have such a wide selection."

Obviously, she thought I patronized the place looking for reading material. Maybe she did volunteer work there. For sure, I wasn't going to say I was over there using the computers because I didn't have one and wanted to find a job that paid more than $10 an hour.

We conversed back and forth for a few minutes and then I knew it was time to move along. "Well, nice meeting you," I said.

"Thank you again for stopping to help," Debbie said. "There's usually a landscape company to take care of the gardens but the person who comes here is out of town. I won't try to do his job in the future." She stuck her hand out again.

So I left, trying to act like I had places to go and people to see. However, that house and that Jag in the driveway and that pretty lady trying to play substitute gardener were the stuff of wet dreams. All the rest of the summer, on my days off, I'd drift past the place, excited when I got a glimpse of Debbie. If she saw me, she'd smile big and wave at me and I'd wave back. Once, I slowed to a crawl and opened the window on the passenger's side.

"How's it going?" I yelled. The Jag was gone from the driveway so I assumed that somebody besides Debbie, most likely a husband, lived in the house and had either driven it someplace or had put it in the garage.

"Just fine!" she called back. "How are you? Found any good books?"

Not knowing where to go from there, I made a sort of meaningless gesture, grinned, and moved along. Much as it gave me pleasure to see the whole package—the house and the car and the lady—I quit going into that neighborhood. If I kept it up, I reasoned, I risked attracting attention as, maybe, a stalker or somebody casing the neighborhood for burglary purposes.

The summer slid by. My job didn't get any more productive and neither did my efforts to find a better one. In early October the Laundromat that I frequented went out of business or moved to some other part of town. There was a place several blocks farther from my apartment and more expensive but what are you going to do? After two weeks worth of dirty clothes had piled up and I was out of clean socks, I figured the time had come.

As I hauled the clothes into the new laundry place, I spotted a familiar profile. Was that Debbie sitting over there paging through one of the old magazines? By God, it was. It was hard to think that people like her ever came to places like this. They called a repair guy or, if their washer wasn't color coordinated with the dryer, they just ordered a new one. In fact, did people like her even do their own laundry?

I walked over to where she sat and said, "Debbie?"

She turned around and yelped out my name. "Steve!" she said. "What are you doing here?"

"Gimme a minute," I said and threw my clothes into the first available machine, then poked in quarters as fast as I could before going over to sit beside her.

"I'm about to wash my dirty clothes," I said, "which fits in real good with my life style—which is not your life style. Is your house too far out for service calls?"

Debbie got what I'd identify as an embarrassed look. "I bet you thought I lived in that house, didn't you? I knew that and just let you think it. I'm sorry. I just worked there. Only I don't anymore."

She was a nice looking woman and I was proud to be talking with her as we sat there watching her underwear and blouses go round and round and saying who we really were. I admitted that my trips to the library were to use the computer and that I likely hadn't read a whole book since my senior year in high school, which was quite some time ago.

A House for Her

She said the folks she worked for had moved away. They promised to give her some great references for the good job she had done as their housekeeper and had made some suggestions that she was following up. She was living with a cousin right now, but that had its drawbacks and she couldn't wait to move on.

We finished our laundry. I loaded her clothes and mine in my old clunker. Her car was in the shop and she wouldn't have the money to get it until her next unemployment check arrived so she had planned to call a taxi to get her back to her cousin's house.

We shared a pizza before I took her home and then we exchanged phone numbers. Of course, one thing led to another and before the winter was over we were sharing a few weekends in my efficiency. The single bed was a drag but we made jokes about it. Sometimes we'd cook a hamburger on some grill we found in a local park, and sometimes we'd go to one of the small, friendly pubs downtown and have a meal. Debbie was one of those rare women who understood a date wasn't necessarily made of money and, without saying anything, she'd pick up her part of the tab. I regretted the necessity but was appreciative and started giving some thought to suggesting we move in together as soon as she found a job. If we pooled our wages, we would both be better off than we presently were and could maybe afford a regular apartment.

One Friday night in early March I picked her up from her cousin's house and she acted so excited that I asked if she'd landed a job.

"Not quite," she said, "but I have a proposition for you. You're going to have to get a little radical with your imagination, but we have a chance to solve all our problems with one decision."

I was skeptical, but all ears. What her proposition came down to was that her former employers had recommended her for what she called a dream job—provided I'd go along with the plan.

This was the basic idea she outlined: An extremely rich couple—part of the one percenters if you will—who lived on an estate just outside of town needed a "couple" to run their household. Debbie would be the housekeeper and maybe do a little light cooking from time to time. Probably not a lot, though, because the couple was often out of town and when they were home and entertained, the entertainment cooking was taken care of by a

51

professional catering company. They also needed a man to look after the household, fixing things from time to time and doing any necessary chauffeuring. There was a Mercedes that was used for that, and the man needed to see that it and other household autos were taken for maintenance. If he needed to pick supplies up for the house, he'd of course have to use the Volvo SUV.

"I can handle that," I said, staring off into space and trying not to go nuts out of sheer ecstasy. "I don't know anything about gardening, though, if they need somebody to do that."

"No problem," said Debbie. "There's a gardener who lives in a little cottage on the grounds. There's also somebody who does the heavy cleaning in the house so that's nothing I'd have to worry about."

"The best part," she added, "is that we'd have a separate apartment of our own in the back of the house. All utilities paid, naturally. We could practically save our entire paychecks. And, come to think of it, you'd have a chance to look into studying for that realtors' license you keep talking about."

"Where do these folks get their money?" I asked. I didn't particularly care but wanted to have a feel for any potential instability.

"As I understand it, from what my former bosses said," Debbie answered, "they're pharmaceutical people. Their company holds the patents on some of those medicines that cost a fortune for just one pill."

"They'll be around for a while," I said. "As long as people get sick and are willing to go broke to get well, they'll do fine."

We went together for our interview, which went pretty well. The people were no spring chickens and that did mean they were a little old-fashioned in their expectations, like what we'd wear and how we served their guests.

"Kind of reminds me of that English thing that was on television a few years back," I said.

"You mean 'Upstairs. Downstairs?" said Debbie. "I suppose so." Then she giggled.

"We'd better get married," I said and Debbie agreed and giggled some more.

We moved into that mansion and it was light years better than I'd seen cruising fancy neighborhoods.

The people who hired us seem satisfied. They want to live someplace in Europe next year, due to some interesting developments in the Euro, and they want us to go there with them to do the same stuff we do here. "Only for a year," they assure us.

Okay by us. Debbie is thrilled out of her mind and if she's happy, so am I. Times are still pretty bad and they say the middle class is wiped out. Maybe it will all turn out like "Upstairs. Downstairs" with everybody saying, "Yes Sir. Yes Madam," to the one percenters. The question is: will there be enough of them to hire all the Debbies and Steves? There are a lot of things to figure out.

PART TWO
A Silent Conspiracy

THE BACK OF GOD'S HEAD

I CAME TO THIS LITTLE CONVENT in northern Missouri when I was about 25 years old. I was after three things: peace, hard work to help me forget some unfortunate early choices, and an occasional moment of beauty. The Bernadette order of nuns offered me that and their small size and location in an obscure part of the country pretty much guaranteed it.

Arriving at peace takes time and still, after three decades, is on my to-do list (although I'm gaining on it). The hard work began immediately. The convent is set on a tract of fertile land that, except for a kitchen garden for our own use, is used for raising strawberries and raspberries for income. Within everyone's memory, the nuns have always taken care of the crops with the help of some of the local inhabitants. During the ripening season, the fruit is trucked over to a small monastery in Kansas that makes incredibly wonderful jam that is sold exclusively in high status department stores in Chicago, St. Louis, and Kansas City. I've tasted it and it's right up there with prayer and good works for holiness.

I went to work in the fields almost immediately after arrival, but just in season. Soon, I was assigned a task that was infinitely harder than dealing with the thorns of raspberry bushes: they decided to make a teacher of me in the classrooms for which the convent is noted. The pupils were as hard to teach as any could be. These days they're known as "special needs" students. Mostly limited as to mental capacity, they can run the gamut from Down's syndrome to severe autism to brain damage due to a myriad of accidental causes. Their learning goes slowly, very slowly.

Some of the Bernadette students come from close-by towns. Their parents bring them in the morning and come after them at the end of the day. Other students are from farther away—even from other states—and they stay in dormitories and are cared for by the Sisters. The care giving has always been done, for the most part, by nuns who are neither academically inclined nor spry though for the strawberry fields. I considered it a blessing that, shortly after my arrival, they figured me for teacher material.

Since it costs quite a bit of money to keep a child in the convent school, the families tend to be prosperous people, either committed to their child's welfare or so happy to have the care done by another entity that they keep hands off and their opinions to themselves. Either way, another blessing.

Jake, at the time I met him, had been attending the convent school for two years. Severely handicapped by his fetal alcohol syndrome, he was nevertheless a joy. He was atypical in some ways. While his problem was easy to identify when one looked at his small, misshapen eyes, he didn't have some of the other characteristics of that problem—the facial anomalies and the small physical size. He actually was rather large for his age and would ultimately grow to stand over six feet. Physically—except for those tell-tale eyes—he was a good looking kid and became a handsome young man.

Born into a poor family in our tiny local community, he had been accepted by the Bernadette's' school on a pro bono basis. Jake's mother was missing in action from the start. Having consumed the alcohol that condemned her son to a lifelong disability, she continued on her merry way after his birth by indulging in just about every illegal activity that she could access. Drug distribution, theft, assault and battery, all were part of her scenario at one time or another. Her father and sister remained in the family home, thus providing Jake with a moderately stable place to live and, after his grandfather died, the state stepped in with a monthly disability check for Jake. He and his aunt lived on that and Jake's mother showed up occasionally, between prison terms. He was always thrilled to see her—then disappointed when she violated parole in some way and got sent back to the prison life she accepted as her real norm.

Jake never mastered articulate speech and depended upon nods and head shakes for a good bit of his communication. When I met him he was about seven years old and assumed to have an extremely low IQ. However, his sunny disposition made up for a lot. His face lit up with pleasure for the most unlikely people and in the most commonplace of circumstances. Grumpy old Sister Matilda, who couldn't find a good word to say about anything, would break out in smiles when she saw Jake coming her way—and no wonder. He would throw his arms around her in a bear hug that was likely one of the few she had experienced in her entire life; she would pat him on the head and once undertook a Novena on his behalf. He had the same effect on almost everyone and other Sisters, inspired by Sister Matilda, began Novenas for Jake as well. Whether there were ever any tangible results is not for me to say but I eventually had cause to believe there were.

A more prosaic person, I had shortcomings when it came to my religious life and beliefs but liked working with Jake and had a suspicion that underneath the garbled speech and naïve behavior there was somewhat of an intellect. He absolutely could not learn to read or write. Still, little experiments that I made, such as reading him test questions and providing an array of possible answers, often resulted in mostly correct choices. He could make sounds approximating "A," "B," "C," and "D" but the other nuns were unimpressed, suggesting that I was hearing what I wanted to hear. Eventually, they went along with my assessment in a moderately accepting sort of way but mostly just because they liked Jake so much and wished him well.

When Jake was nine, somebody gave him a dog. If he was a happy person before, that dog gave him joy without bound. The dog was of no particular breed or color but sort of ginger hued, with a medium sized body, scrubby short hair, and perky ears that took in all the noises that Jake made and then made sense of them. His tail had been docked but the little bit he had left was in perpetual motion, especially in response to Jake. One of the locals named the mutt "Bowser," which Jake accepted. He couldn't say "Bowser," the sound coming out as "Bah-wah," but it worked for the dog. I happened to be in the garden one day when Jake and his dog were wandering through and Sister Clara, who's a trifle condescending, asked Jake, "How is Bah-wah today?" She hadn't expected an answer at all—certainly not the fury in Jakes's voice when he screamed, "NO! Bah-wah!" He couldn't say "Bowser" but he certainly expected to hear it.

A few years later, decisions had to be made about Jake and whether he should be bused to the high school in Cornwallis, the county seat, for further attempts at education and socialization. His aunt didn't really care and never came to parent conferences so the nuns decided to buy him some clothes from the convent funds and pay whatever other expenses were indicated, then see to it that he got on the bus each week day. It was a good decision; Jake soon learned to get himself on the bus and in addition to his special education classes in the Cornwallis school took pleasure in helping out the basketball team. He couldn't exactly play, since he was easily confused and tended to run to the wrong side of the gym when the ball was in motion, but his sunny disposition led to friendships with the kids on the team and the coach. He was encouraged to bring out the equipment before each ball game and for this he got to wear a team suit and a satin jacket that sported the school letter—an outfit that gave him immense pride.

Poor Bowser spent Monday through Friday crouched at the roadside where the school bus stopped each afternoon. When Jake came home, both he and the dog went into paroxysms of delight. When Jake stayed late because of the basketball schedule, Bowser was so dejected and lonely that I often asked one of our farm workers to take him to a nearby shed for food and shelter. Bowser would go, reluctantly, but knew the sound of the vehicle coming to bring Jake home and would bound out in a rapture of welcoming leaps and tail wagging.

It was hard for the pastor of St. Bernadette's little parish to know quite what to do regarding Jake's religious milestones. Each time the yearly confirmation rite was about to take place, the question came up if Jake should be included. He had been a participant in many of the religion classes but nobody knew whether anything said in them had taken root in his mind.

Father Louis decided to settle the question once and for all about the time Jake turned 15. Having heard that the boy might be capable of a few intellectual choices, he asked me if I'd bring him over to the rectory for a bit of an examination. I complied, wondering what the outcome might be. The diocese tended to send St. Bernadette elderly priests who would be eligible for retirement after a short term in our community; after a few years they were taken away, sent to a retirement destination, and another, similar priest would come for a brief stay.

Father Louis was a meek little man who was given to small noises that emanated unbidden from his mouth and intestines. He couldn't help it, if in fact he actually knew it was happening, but at least he wasn't going to do the macho thing on Jake.

"Do you love God?" he sweetly asked the boy.

I repeated the question in a way that begged for a positive answer.

Jake gave a tentative nod—too tentative to satisfy Father Louis, who wasn't sure the boy understood what he was being asked. He made an unfortunate decision to amplify the question. Nodding toward Bowser, who was sitting on the rectory porch waiting for Jake, he asked, "Who do you love most—Bowser or God?"

No need to think that one out. Jake responded emphatically and heartily, "Bah-wah!"

Father Louis was confounded but decided he hadn't made himself clear. "We must love the Lord our God above all else, as you have been taught. Now, think hard and answer carefully, Who do you love more—God or Bowser?"

Jake looked perplexed and a tiny frown line appeared on his always cheery face. "BAH-WAH!" he said, very loudly as if Father Louis might have hearing problems.

The religious examination was a bust and the little priest evidently made some internal decision that was not comfortable. "Take him home," he said to me. "There's no use going on with this. He obviously doesn't comprehend what he's being asked or what to answer."

I had my own opinion but knew enough to keep it to myself. "Shall we assume," I asked in as humble a voice as I could muster, "that since God loves his children — and this young man will be a child forever—that he meets with His favor?"

A brief nod, a small fart, a swallowed belch, and Father Louis opened the rectory door to dismiss us. After that, Jake was included as part of the newly confirmed. He was around a lot longer than Father Louis was and went to Holy Communion on some occasions when, as Sister Matilda said, "the Spirit moved him." I'm sure he wouldn't have had the slightest idea what a Confessional was for, but all of the St. Bernadette congregation, those in Holy Orders and those without, retained a sort of silent conspiracy regarding Jake and his religious parameters.

The convent sat beautifully on the grounds, with the fields stretching southward behind the cemetery where generations of Sisters were laid to rest. Our local peace and quiet was mildly interrupted at times by traffic on the narrow, two-lane road that ran east to Cornwallis and several miles west toward a super highway. But, as long as it didn't get too bad, we tuned it out.

I had a favorite perch out of sight of the convent where I sometimes watched sunsets. After all, I had come to the Bernadettes hoping for occasional moments of beauty and, although I knew my self-indulgence should have sent me to the Confessional many times, it tended to leave me unrepentant.

On one particular autumn dusk, I watched the sky turn incredible shades of gold and rose as the phenomena known as "Jacob's ladders" filled the western vista. It's no wonder, I thought to myself, that a whole review of civilizations stretching back to the Beginning, made up stories about what those rays of light signified. Not hard, I reflected, to imagine bands of deities rising and descending in the incredible light.

It was irritating when the noise of an automobile rose to defile the spectacle. Turning my head for a moment, I could see Jake farther down the road, fishing rod in hand, and was glad to see he was walking on the edge, a safety precaution that he'd been taught years earlier. Fishing was something he could do by himself, as he developed into his mid-teens. Bowser always accompanied him, perhaps drawn by a conglomeration of delicious smells to the little creek that ran through a nearby grove of trees. At the moment I watched, Jake paused and, missing Bowser at his side, called out, "Bah-wah! Bah-wah!"

Bowser came running out of the stand of trees and toward Jake at the exact moment when the noisy automobile sped past the convent grounds. It caught the dog as he crossed the road, hitting the animal hard enough to throw him several feet. Predictably, the car's careless driver didn't falter for a second and the vehicle was soon out of sight around a bend in the road. For the next few seconds, I went numb, hearing Jake's anguished screams as if they were far away.

Then, struggling to find a shred of physical and mental composure, I prepared to go to Jake and deal with the situation as best I could.

Somebody beat me to it.

A man, a vagrant from what I could see, had emerged from somewhere—maybe the trees— and was bending over Bowser. His back was toward me, so my split-second impression was of a counter culture type, long unkempt hair pulled back by a strip of bandana and wearing a pair of patched jeans and a ragged tee.

Since I'd seen the hit that tossed Bowser into a limp pile at the side of the road, I had made the immediate assumption that he had been killed. Jake would be inconsolable and I would have to ask for lots of help in dealing with the tragic scenario.

My assumption was in error. The vagrant in the road lifted Bowser in his arms and carried him over to Jake. As the boy reached out for his beloved dog, I was astonished to see Bowser shake himself and that irrepressible tail begin to wag with its customary delight at reunion with his dearest friend.

By the time I took all of that in, the vagrant had disappeared. I didn't see him go, but thought he had probably taken a shortcut through the wooded area in order to get over to the four-lane highway where he could get a hitch. When I got to Jake, he was already back in his normal good spirits and both he and Bowser greeted me happily. Knowing that neither of them would be able to talk about the close call with the speeding car, I went back to the convent for evening devotions and thanked God and all the saints for Bowser's—and Jake's—reprieve. Then I made a small resolution to keep the episode to myself so questions wouldn't be asked.

We aged, all of us. Sister Matilda went to her eternal rest in the convent cemetery. Sister Clair became the principal of the Bernadette school for special needs children, and I welcomed a reassignment to manage the convent's finances—including the cultivation, picking and transporting of the strawberries and raspberries to their destination in Kansas.

Jake aged, too, and at 35 worked in the fields from time to time and enjoyed special status at the convent. The young students thought he was wonderful because he was as kind and joyous with them as with everyone else. They enjoyed Bowser, too, and the dog was gentle with them, even when they pulled his stump of a tail and poked at him with disregard for his dignity.

Jake had aged from 14 to 35 in traditional male appearance. He grew whiskers that someone, maybe the parish priests, showed him how to shave. Of a tall stature, he had learned to temper his outgoing enthusiasm into a relatively decorous demeanor that became him. Every year that passed, I grew more certain that there were normal brain processes hiding under the façade of the developmental problems caused by his fetal alcohol syndrome. He would have been lost without Bowser, however.

Did I say Bowser? Yes, I did.

Bowser, contrary to the rest of us, did not age. Counting back over the years, it was well over twenty years since he had been hit by the car that sped past the convent and he had definitely been several years old at the time. Do dogs live to be thirty or more years of age? Not yet, according to any information about canine longevity that I could find. Additionally, Bowser remained as frisky as he'd been as a pup, ready to accompany Jake wherever he went, and always with his stump of a tail in perpetual motion.

People in the Bernadette parish didn't notice. If they did, they probably assumed that Jake had had a series of dogs, all more or less looking the same. I once heard Sister Clair ask Jake the name of his new dog. Jake looked puzzled and answered her as he had years before, "BAH-WAH!" Sister Clair turned away, no doubt with pity for the young man who, she thought, didn't know his original dog from a latecomer.

In his thirty-fifth year, Jake fell from a barn loft that was a mile or two from the Bernadette parish. Someone had hired him for a couple of days to help out with farm chores and he was in the loft throwing down hay bales. He tripped over one of the bales and, when he hit the ground, his head smashed against a piece of farm equipment that stood nearby. Mercifully, he died instantly.

His aunt put on a moderately convincing show of sorrow and the rest of us were genuinely grief stricken. Jake was part of the community and his handicaps had made him eternally conspicuous. People over in Cornwallis — who remembered him from his basketball days—sorrowed as well.

Father Steve, who was the fourth or fifth priest since Father

Louis to be assigned to St. Bernadette, cornered me and said, "I have to do a little homily at Jake's funeral and have been told that you know him better than anyone. Do you have any topic suggestions?" It didn't take much more than a minute for me to reply, "The Beatitudes come to my mind. Something like, 'Blessed are the pure in heart for they shall see God.'"

Jake, wearing his satin letter jacket from the Cornwallis school, was buried in the part of the Bernadette's cemetery reserved for local folks. Father Steve's words made us cry because everyone who had known Jake knew him for the beautiful person he was.

A few people remarked that Bowser was nowhere to be seen after Jake's death. I think they half-expected the dog to be present at the funeral as a mourner and hang out afterward in the vicinity of Jake's grave. Jake's aunt, when questioned, said Bowser hadn't shown up at home although she had thought he would and kept a dish of dog food out on the back porch.

Those expectations were not mine. Bowser's job was finished. My memory often slipped back to the sunset I'd watched years before and the vagrant who had come from nowhere, bathed in the light of the Jacob's ladders, to restore Bowser to Jake's anxious arms. Had Jake, when he looked up to take his dog from the stranger, seen the face of God?

I thought I knew and I was a little jealous. But, recalling the untidy hair tied back with a strip of soiled bandana, I knew that—at least—I had seen the back of God's head.

A PENNY POSTCARD

"SHE HAS THE BEST LOOKING teeth in Millwell," said Doc Pinster as he leaned over the patient in his dental chair.

A moment before he had looked up to check the latest action on Main Street. His second floor window was a ready-made vantage point and just about anyone who came into view was familiar. The person he'd just seen was Miss Markay, local seamstress and semi-recluse. He could have provided a thumbnail sketch about most of Millwell's local residents but the Markay woman was pretty much an unknown. She certainly wasn't one of his patients so his assessment of her teeth was an independent conclusion based on a chance encounter in the local grocery store when they both reached for the same bottle of milk. She had smiled an apology although she certainly didn't owe him one and he had quickly withdrawn his claim on the milk.

Manny Streeter, the patient in the chair, could only raise an eyebrow. The appliance that gurgled away in his mouth, plus the restriction of his head, kept him immobile. Still, without looking, he was aware of whom Doc was speaking.

Through the day-to-day gossip of his post office patrons, he knew that Miss Markay had come to town many years before and lived by herself in two rooms over what was called "the electric shop," a place where people went to pay their monthly utility bills and which carried an assortment of nice looking lamps.

He also knew that Miss Markay seldom descended the steep stairs that led to Main Street. She had very little money, he had heard, and used most of it to buy simple items that could be cooked on her two-burner hot plate. In the wintertime, a few dairy items could be stored on the sills just outside her windows, but without refrigeration her meals during warm weather were largely limited to loaves of bread and whatever came sealed in cans. She earned the money for her meager food and cheap rent by altering and sewing garments for the small number of people who wanted the service.

One of those people was Doc Pinster's lady friend, Shirley Spence. One of the few single women in Millwell with a skilled job, except for schoolteachers (who usually left town in the summer), Shirley sat in the telephone office most days saying, "Number please," to local residents. People often dropped by to pay their phone bills and gossip a bit but never got any information from Shirley because she took seriously the privacy code laid down by Bell Central.

She and Doc often went to one or another of the nearby county seat towns to buy groceries, have dinner and, perhaps, see a picture show. Obviously, therefore, Shirley needed a wider variety of dresses than did most of Millwell's women. A lot of men were away in the service of the United States, fighting Germany or Japan. That left Shirley as one of the few women who had dates and having dates meant more attention must be paid to one's wardrobe. Consequently, she took lengths of fabric to Miss Markay's rooms with some regularity. In the beginning she also took a variety of patterns—mostly variations on simple shirtwaist styles—but Miss Markay quickly made it known that she could manage very well without them. She had Shirley's measurements memorized and Shirley felt, rather than knew, that the dressmaker's efforts bordered on fashion designer work. A pleat here, a gore there, an unexpected drape to the sleeve, an occasional off-center neckline punctuated by a charming rosette—no Des Moines department store dress rack could match what Miss Markay achieved despite Shirley's inexpensive and unexciting fabrics.

Doc bragged about it to Manny now, as he relinquished him from the dental chair and both turned to watch the seamstress cross the street to the grocery store. "Shirley has a few figure flaws," he confided, "but you'd never know it, thanks to that lady's skill."

Manny flushed with embarrassment. He had never looked hard enough at Shirley to discern any figure flaws and wondered how Doc knew about them. To all appearances, all three of them—Doc, himself, and Shirley—were single people living exemplary lives. Shirley lived in a house located near the telephone office, Doc lived in rooms behind his office, and Manny, the local postmaster, lived in rooms over the post office—all of them therefore in close proximity to their livelihoods. Neither Manny nor Doc welcomed visitors, including one another, to his personal quarters. In Millwell-speak, each minded his own business and steered clear of being objects of small town gossip. Manny never paid Doc for his three-month appointments unless there was a genuine dental problem and those were rare because Manny brushed his teeth after every meal, used floss and seldom ate sweets. They simply used the frequent dental checkups to catch up on observations about the small town in which they lived.

Manny had some figure flaws of his own. He was essentially a pear shape and had been since his difficult youth when school bullies had addressed him as "Lard Ass." This condition was made worse by the long hours spent sitting on a stool just inside the service window in the post office, doling out stamps and postcards. For years, he'd had to buy his pants in a large size at a Des Moines men's store that had a good tailor, one capable of nipping in the waist and conducting camouflage with pleats.

Hearing Doc's praise of Miss Markay, he thought wistfully of the money he could save by taking his tailoring business to her but, on second thought, how could he go to a woman for this intimate service? Not that she was at all frightening to look at. He saw her as a female well into her sixties, plainly dressed, who wore her hair pulled back and secured by a hair net. With very little experience in rating feminine attributes, he shrugged off Doc's praise for Miss Markay's marvelous teeth, supposedly (according to Doc) encased in a patrician facial contour. She was, for Manny, an exceedingly plain woman without one iota of prettiness.

He had, in fact, spoken to her once, nearly a year before. A letter for her had arrived in the post office. It had no return address but "Madeleine Markay, Millwell, Iowa" was written in refined script in the precise place where a proper address should present itself. Manny had particularly noticed it because the handwriting was elegant, similar to Manny's own writing. The letter was postmarked "Dubuque," an Iowa town on the other side of the state with which he had little familiarity.

Miss Markay had no post office box and never came by to see if she had received any mail but Manny felt responsible for seeing to it that she got this letter within an appropriate number of days. He would have considered climbing the stairs to her rooms an audacious act but took the letter over to the electric shop to be given to her by the manager when she next emerged.

As luck would have it, Miss Markay came down the stairs to

Main Street at that precise moment so he said, "Miss Markay, you have some mail," and she said, "Thank you," and that was that. He reflected, at the time, that her diction and tone were uncommonly melodious for a Millwell person—but how much could one tell from two simple words?

A postcard arrived some months later and shortly after Manny's dental appointment. It also was simply addressed to "Madeleine Markay, Millwell, Iowa," and had the same Dubuque postmark. Manny retained some memory of the handwriting on the previously received letter because of its old-school penmanship and its similarity to his own. He now judged that the same person had addressed both card and letter. Doc might evaluate people by their teeth but Manny thought penmanship a better measurement and was inclined to assess most persons by their cursive.

Expecting graceful phrases, he turned the card over to see what it said. (Manny often read postcards, although he would have chopped off one of his hands before admitting that to anyone.)

The message was unsigned and its content was not in keeping with the handwriting. It curtly said, "Cannot permit you to return home. Traitors to the family are not welcome."

What to do? Manny's sense of civility would not allow him to leave the postcard with the electric store manager — who would inevitably spread its content around town—but he hesitated even more at delivering it personally. He might, he thought, have to ask Myrtle Schaefer, who substituted in the post office when Manny was on vacation — as well as helping out on Wednesdays and Saturdays — to take the card up the narrow, dark stairs to Miss Markay's rooms. Myrtle would insufferably pretend a time crunch when asked, but she knew where her bread was buttered and surely wouldn't broadcast the card's contents to gossip-hungry Millwell.

It turned out that his concern was unnecessary. A morning or two later, while he was still waiting for Myrtle to pick up and deliver the post card, the first person who came into the post office stopped at his window and said, "How about that Markay murder? Poor lady found strangled in her own apartment! Who's next? Somebody's out to get us!"

The newspaper published in the county seat and subscribed to by a number of Millwell citizens had a big headline that said, in a self-conscious blitz of capital Ms, "MAIN STREET MURDER! MILLWELL MYSTERY!"

Six post office visitors later, Manny knew that one of the town ladies had gone to Miss Markay's rooms with a winter coat that needed alteration and, when her persistent knocks went unheeded, had cautiously pushed open the unlocked door. Seeing the seamstress sprawled on the floor, she had run hastily down the stairs and yelled the information to everyone on Main who was within earshot.

The electric store manager corralled half a dozen people and all of them quickly ascended the steps. Determining that the lady was not only dead but had obviously been dead for more than a day, he summoned the sheriff from the county seat who, in turn, summoned the general practitioner who served as county coroner. Death by strangulation was the conclusion, a terrifying thought indeed. Miss Markay had been choked to death by someone's bare hands. There were bruises to prove it.

The sheriff, never very professional at best, conducted a tiny little investigation. First, he cross examined the would-be customer who had first found the deceased Miss Markay until that lady broke down in hysterical sobs. The only other person he thought might have any information at all was Shirley Spence, and that only because telephone operators supposedly knew everything. Shirley said Miss Markay had come to the telephone office a couple of weeks before and asked about making a long distance call. However, she had decided she couldn't afford the cost and had gone away. Shirley found it unnecessary to tell the sheriff that Miss Markay had, on the same occasion, given her a note saying that she, Miss Markay, was sorry to inform Miss Spence that she was going to return to her home town in a couple of weeks on the Greyhound bus that stopped on Main Street three times a week and that Miss Spence would have to find a new dressmaker.

Shirley passed this information on to Doc and it was then passed on to Manny when Doc came into the post office to pick up his mail. "Why tell that idiot of a so-called sheriff anything?" Doc said. "Nothing would happen except the county paper would run more of those stupid headlines."

Doc had a theory connected with the murder. He said it hadn't been done by a local person and had undoubtedly happened on band concert night. Any other time, day or night, everybody would see an out-of-county car parked on Main Street. On Saturday nights, however, every parking space was filled and there were cars parked in the alleys and on side streets as well. Easy enough, he said, for a strange car and unfamiliar face to go temporarily unnoticed.

Manny thought Doc might be correct in blaming an outsider but wasn't about to reveal his own exclusive information that a somewhat threatening postcard had arrived for Miss Markay from Dubuque, that there had not been time to deliver it, and that he still had it. It also occurred to him that he was likely the only person in town who knew Miss Markay's first name was the romantic sounding "Madeleine."

When Shirley came in to get her mail, looking astonishingly fashionable for a week day in Millwell, he overcame his usual shyness about talking to her and asked about the note she had received from the deceased dressmaker. Shirley said Miss Markay's handwriting was just so pretty that she wouldn't have turned it over to the sheriff for anything in the world.

"It wouldn't have told him anything," she said, readjusting a pearl earring, "I'll just keep it in my mementos to remember her by. She was so sweet and talented!"

Manny surprised himself with his next remark.

"You know," he said, "handwriting is sort of a hobby with me, especially that old fashioned kind that some of us were once taught in parochial schools by perfectionist nuns. I would very much like to see Miss Markay's penmanship and study it a little bit. Would you be willing to let me see the note? I'll be very careful with it and return it to you in a day or two."

Shirley, surprised at Manny's unexpected request, said that she guessed that would be okay and she'd bring it in. Then she hurried off to tell Doc and a few others that, guess what, Manny Streeter had grown up attending a religious school and maybe that's why he was so stiff and proper.

Manny's theory focused on the penny postcard from Dubuque. Obviously, Miss Markay was in touch with somebody there who didn't want her to come back. If she had written to anyone in that town, he would have seen it when he stamped the outgoing mail. She had to have telephoned her intentions to Dubuque—but how, especially if she hadn't made a call from the town telephone office? Actually, that was pretty easy to figure out. He had once heard that when Miss Markay needed to call a customer to say she had finished with that person's sewing project, the folks in the downstairs electric company office let her use their telephone. Miss Markay had simply sneaked in a free call or two to somebody in Dubuque and nobody heard her because polite Iowa folks like the electric shop people would have stepped away to give her privacy. Shirley wouldn't have picked up on it because the phone in the electric store was used all the time for any number of boring reasons not worth listening to. And the phone bill itself was sent to a central office in Des Moines, not to the Millwell location.

After Manny received the note that Miss Markay had written to Shirley, he could hardly wait for closing time at the post office and his escape to his upstairs apartment. Barely pausing for an abridged supper, he sat at his desk and put the Dubuque postcard and Miss Markay's note side by side. He then got out his own note paper and proceeded to list similarities and differences on a separate sheet of paper. He noted that, one, the message was written on a page of three-hole punched notebook paper. It was written in medium blue ink by a not very good writing implement, probably one of those cheap fountain pens sold by the dozen in the drug store and used by a majority of the population for both business and personal reasons. (Here, he lovingly patted his shirt pocket where dwelt his own expensive Mont Blanc pen that he had once paid for with nearly a month's wages.)

The penmanship of the note was superb. He could hardly have done as well himself and, certainly, there were few people in Millwell who could write as beautifully. It was in a style that came close to calligraphy, without yielding to the extremely sweeping flourishes of that art form. Instead, it was a relic of the day when elaborate writing was still taught in schools and a border of perfectly formed letters adorned classroom walls. Bottles of ink rested in ink holes on student desks and, when pen and ink were called for, straight pens were dipped into them. The bottle contents occasionally spilled out onto schoolroom floors, to the despair of teachers and school janitors, but these were to be expected. Pupils with extra skills in handwriting were awarded appreciative grades on their report cards. (He, himself, had been the only boy in his grade school whose handwriting had lived up to that standard. It was the cause of a few accolades and he had lovingly practiced penmanship for many hours at home when he needed a break from reading his way through the Des Moines library system.)

Manny retrieved the undelivered postcard from Dubuque and held it next to Miss Markay's note to Shirley. Ah, the writing was similar, very similar, perhaps indicating that both were done by people who had learned to write during the same time frame and, possibly, had been taught by the same person. Were the writers related?

One difference between the writing samples stood out. The postcard was written with bolder strokes. Where Miss Markay's writing was delicate and feminine, the writer of the post card had pressed more heavily on the pen. Additionally, the words evidenced the sort of flow one might expect from a more expensive writing implement.

A man! A man, thought Manny, had surely written the postcard. Its message that traitors to the family would not be welcome most assuredly was masculine and men were, also, much more likely to value a good pen. Women, Manny had noticed, didn't put much importance on what implement they used to write — whatever it was that women wrote.

And now he was afflicted with a mental image of Miss Markay as he had seen her last and then as she was described by the people who found her dead. Someone had put their hands around her throat and strangled her to death. Someone who was still out there— probably in Dubuque—and was not only getting away with murder but might kill again.

Manny tucked the postcard into an attaché case that he seldom had an excuse to use and then sat at his desk until long past his bedtime, copying and recopying Miss Markay's note to Shirley. It wasn't particularly difficult to lighten his writing until it took on a feminine look, but it reflected the superior strokes caused by his cherished pen. A true facsimile would have to be done by one of those cheap drug store pens.

He shrugged and tucked his efforts into his attaché case along with the post card. Perhaps this was silly, but he'd not have another chance to compare the two writing samples. Tomorrow, without

70

fail, he'd have to return Miss Markay's note to Shirley, making some off-hand comment about how people certainly didn't write like that anymore, that it was a lost art.

Dubuque was nearly all the way across the state from Millwell. Manny had never been there and knew nothing about it except its location on the Mississippi River. While he was convinced that someone should go there and see if there were any Markays related to the late seamstress, he was reluctant about electing himself to the task. On the other hand, he knew in his bones that it really was up to him to do the research. Interest in the murder was dying down fast for lack of evidence and only Shirley Spence exhibited any concern over Miss Markay's passing.

The general consensus in Millwell was that the murder was a robbery attempt gone bad. The citizenry was more careful for a few days about locking doors and the town's night watchman made an effort to stay awake and vigilant instead of taking his usual long naps in the back of the hardware store. And, naturally, any local citizen who owned a gun took it down from the closet shelf on which it was stored and gave it a good cleaning.

Manny considered the logistics of travelling to Dubuque.

These days, all buses were filled to overflowing with servicemen being shuttled from one Army or Navy base to another. Much as he would like to save his scarce gas rationing coupons and wear and tear on his Chevrolet, going by Greyhound was a terrible idea. Manny shuddered at the thought of sharing seats, bathrooms and lunch counters with the many GIs who undoubtedly would be on unsupervised behavior and thus similar in action to the rude males with whom he had gone to school. He bought war bonds each month; he mourned quietly, within himself, for the families who lost their sons and hung gold stars in their windows; he deplored the slaughter and mayhem that gripped the world. But he would not travel in the company of uncouth young males.

He would have to drive himself.

Fortunately, Highway 20 would make the drive uncomplicated. Assuming it would take most of a day to get to Dubuque and a second day to hunt for a possible relative of Miss Markay who could supply information about her, then a day to drive back to Millwell, he was probably looking at two nights in a hotel. Dubuque was large

71

enough to have some of those, he assumed, as well as having a number of nice restaurants.

It would be a regular vacation, especially if he maintained the right attitude, drove slowly, investigated points of interest along the way, and perhaps took a few pictures with his Brownie Reflex camera which he used all too infrequently.

Thus motivated, he set out. But points of interest were scarce on Highway 20. Beyond Fort Dodge, a town with which Manny was already somewhat familiar, the road stretched endlessly between fields of corn. Small towns cropped up along the way but their streets were mere variations on Millwell's, existing only to supply the folks who lived within practical travelling distance. They had evolved when their stores were accessed by horses and wagons and, even though little change was going on right now, they would likely change some more after the war was over.

One thing that would not change—at this moment and possibly forever—was the endless range of corn fields; Manny found little reason to point his Brownie. In Iowa City, a painter named Grant Wood had made a reputation for himself with his vistas of rural Iowa. Manny did not care for the style, finding it wooden, or for Wood's subject matter. He preferred landscapes with mountains and lakes and had an album in which he had pasted the photos he had taken on trips to more scenic parts of the United States. The walls of his rooms over the Millwell post office held prints of several nicely framed vistas. One of those pictured a gondola in Venice that was occupied by a lustily singing oarsman. What possible interest could any artist have in a rural expanse made up of endless rows of corn and men on tractors who rode up and down those rows?

Once he was resigned to the tedious landscape, he centered his attention on finding a restaurant where he could eat lunch. The main drag of one of the towns yielded a glimpse of a plate glass window that had R E S T A U R A N T nicely painted across its breadth. Obviously, a sign painter had once gone through town; Manny thought that a restaurant that had paid to have such an expert sign might also take some care with its cooking.

Once inside, his guess proved semi-correct. The horde of people eating lunch appeared, from their dress, to be the kind of businessmen who might work in the local bank or furniture store, or even in a small hospital. Manny sat at the counter and chose the meatloaf special. When it arrived in front of him swimming in brown gravy, he shuddered a little but ate most of it and paid at the cash register when finished, courteously declining the offer of a nicely packaged toothpick.

The remaining distance to Dubuque continued to offer much the same outlook. Corn rows. Barns. Barbed wire fences. Once in a while a pasture with cows or a weathered looking farmhouse. He was relieved when a sign along the road said Dubuque was only ten miles farther.

And what a shock that was, when he achieved its outskirts. This was like no Iowa town he had ever seen. There were hills! Denison had some hills, as did Sioux City and other western Iowa spots, but Dubuque had hills with a capital H and bluffs, too. Additionally, the Mississippi River lapped at its edge.

Manny had learned in grade school about the travels of Father Marquette and his companion, Joliet, as they explored the huge river, bringing their French interests to the area. If he had thought about it before, he would have dug out his set of encyclopedias to refresh his knowledge, but maybe that would have spoiled the fun. This was going to be—nearly—like having an adventure in a far-off and exotic place.

Coaxing his Chevy up and down the hills until he found Dubuque's commercial area, the first thing to do in this late afternoon hour was find a hotel. And that he did, based somewhat on the hotel having its own garage space and somewhat because it had a very nice restaurant located just off the lobby. Not a coffee shop, mind you, but a restaurant with white tablecloths and proper waiters. Later, when shown to a table by a beyond-draft-age gentleman, Manny felt as if he was doing precisely what he was destined to do—taking part in the ritual of fine living shown on movie screens and described in the novels of Henry James.

Torn between a choice of chicken breast with mushrooms and ham with raisin sauce, he decided on the ham. It still being Iowa, on the map at least, there was no wine to be quaffed, but his Pepsi came in a crystal goblet and his coffee in a bone china cup. The ham was the best he had ever eaten and he topped it off with a slice of plum tart that was nothing like the popular dessert offerings at a Millwell church supper.

Afterward, gorged to the point of indigestion, he sat in the lobby reading a local newspaper and watching the well-dressed people who came and went. Then, because he was very tired from his long car trip and lavish dinner, he retired to his room and was soothed to sleep by a ceiling fan that agreeably stirred the warm air.

The next morning, somewhat burdened by the immense dinner he had eaten, not to mention the gravy covered meatloaf he'd had for lunch, he bypassed the hotel's dining room in favor of a slice of toast and some grapefruit juice in the coffee shop. The smart thing to do first, he decided, was to walk about in the uptown area bordering the hotel. As he walked, he would not only get a look at this interesting city of Dubuque but, additionally, his head would clear and his digestive tract would calm.

A query at the desk as to points of interest within the vicinity brought an enthusiastic response. "Well, Sir," said the person he addressed, "you just have to take a look at our post office and courthouse."

"Are they in the same area?" asked Manny, with something of alarm. He had calluses on the bottoms of his feet and consequently was not a good walker.

"You might say." said the desk clerk. "The post office is on the first floor and the courthouse is on the second floor. The building was finished about ten years ago and Dubuque is mighty proud of it. You might even catch a tour if you get over there at the right time."

A post office fine enough to merit tours? Manny could not imagine it although, of course, he'd seen a few nice ones here and there during his travels.

The Dubuque post office/courthouse turned out to be truly splendid. A three-story, cream colored building with a cupola rising another story above, it was awe inspiring. There were no tours this morning, said a woman who looked as if she would know and Manny was reluctant to ask where the chief postmaster's office was located. Perhaps if he knew, he could stop by for a little visit, one postmaster to another. This Dubuque postmaster would definitely not be seated on a stool in front of a service window, but he might be amenable to meeting a colleague.

But probably not, Manny reluctantly decided. In a post office such as this, with rose-grey marble wainscoting and lavishly painted murals, important decisions and meetings would surely take up the time of its chief official. With a final, envious thought about how much salary a Dubuque post master would be paid, he stepped outside. He was not here to sight see, he was here to locate Miss Markay's family and, possibly, determine the identity of her murderer.

He needed to talk to someone who knew something of the city's families and that would entail making the acquaintance of a complete stranger. He knew, from the depths of his being, that if there was anything he was not good at, it was talking to complete strangers without a very good reason for doing so. There had to be a rationale for approaching a person, perhaps interrupting that person at an important task or keeping him from his necessary schedule. (Manny thought only of the rigors of approaching a man. Approaching a strange woman was unimaginable. Not even if he was bleeding to death and needed a tourniquet.)

At last he thought of a well-mannered way to talk to a stranger without putting that person out. He would go to a men's clothing store, buy a pair of pants, and have the pants tailored to fit him. Conversation would be indigenous to the procedure.

No sooner thought than acted upon. The downtown area held a couple of well-known department stores and at least two men's stores. Manny chose one of the men's stores because, judging from the window display of fine clothing, it would surely have a tailor on the premises.

The shop obviously catered to professional men. Its prices and the courteous mien of its attending clerk proved that. Looking through the racks of dress pants, Manny got back some of the sense of wellbeing he had lost while wondering about the Dubuque postmaster's salary. He was not one to be pretentious, but he had nevertheless enjoyed a feeling of sophistication last night as he sat at a white damask covered table in the hotel dining room, sipping his Pepsi in its crystal goblet. Buying a pair of pants fit for a prosperous professional man was an appropriate act.

Now, returned to his state of grace, he selected a pair of pants in the improbable size needed for his rear end and with great dignity said to the clerk, who had maintained a discreet distance from him, "These will do very well. I do need a certain amount of tailoring to make them fit. I trust you have someone who does alterations."

With a look of ever so faint astonishment, as if the clerk had no idea what kind of tailoring Manny might need—then followed by an expression of total assurance—the man said, "Oh yes! Our Mr. Gates is one of the very best tailors to be found this side of Chicago. As it happens, he is on the premises this morning. Shall I introduce you?"

Mr. Gates, when approached in his little realm in back of the store, was somewhat of a disappointment. Manny anticipated a person of great poise, rather English in his bearing—reminiscent, in fact, of persons such as the Duke of Windsor. What he got was a wiry little guy with a faded anchor tattoo on one of his wrists. The imprint of the anchor had likely taken place somewhere around the time of World War I, judging from Mr. Gates' crinkled visage. His accent, far from British, held echoes of the Great Plains.

"What can I do ya' for?" he asked, as the store clerk gently gave Manny's choice of trousers into his hands.

Fumbling for a regal explanation of the incongruity between his dimensions, Manny was interrupted as Mr. Gates held up the pants, viewed the size and then visually scanned Manny's physique. Undoubtedly used to such discrepancies, the tailor bade Manny to drop his pants and don the new ones. He got busy with chalk and pins, saying, "Um hum, oh yes, okay, well then." So efficient was he that Manny despaired of a chance for conversation—the very reason why he was buying a too-expensive pair of pants in the first place.

He began rather tremulously. "Have you lived in Dubuque for long?"

Taking a pin or two from his mouth, Mr. Gates said, courteously but briefly, "Quite a few years." Then he popped the pins back in, indicating the end of the discussion.

Manny tried again. "I live across the state. Here on business. Promised an acquaintance that I'd look up her family. Do you by chance know of a family by the name of Markay?"

Mr. Gates sputtered just enough to make Manny worry that the man had swallowed one of his pins.

"Nope."

That was it. Just "Nope." Case closed. End of discussion.

"When do you need these pants?" asked Mr. Gates.

. His feelings bruised by the brush-off, Manny's posture and voice were stiff. "I hope to return home tomorrow. Is that too soon for you?"

"Day after is as soon as I can do it. That's not convenient for me but seeing as you're travelling, I'll try to accommodate you," said Mr. Gates.

One more day in Dubuque! That meant an extra night in the hotel, more meals, and a long distance call to Millwell to make sure Myrtle Schaefer could continue to cover for him in the Millwell post office. Just as well, perhaps. Today was half over and his investigation hadn't even started. Manny swallowed hard. He needed a plan and it would take the rest of the day to think of one.

With regret, he skipped lunch. By dinnertime, he thought, his belly would perhaps no longer be doing flip-flops. Retrieving the Chevrolet from the hotel garage, he drove around Dubuque admiring the historic area with its fine houses dating back for who knows how long. He then drove along the river shore, which he thought tough and decrepit, not in keeping with Dubuque as it otherwise presented itself. This, in turn, was counterbalanced by the plethora of beautiful churches and church institutions that were everywhere.

His day, thus far, did have its downside and he was so tired that a nap would be a great luxury. His pleasant hotel room, with its agreeably turning ceiling fan, was a temptation to which he yielded. After all, was he not treating himself to a few days of vacation? When, if ever, was he able to indulge in a nap?

When Manny awoke, he was startled to see that he had slept away most of the afternoon and it was dinner time. Much as he longed to return to the beautiful dining room with its white tablecloths and respectful waiters, he decided his budget and digestion would fare better if he skipped it. A large department store stood opposite to the hotel and he knew that large department stores always had a relatively satisfactory and economical restaurant. That is where he would dine this evening. Tomorrow evening would be open to another decision.

This particular department store restaurant was set up as a cafeteria. One pushed one's tray along, supplying it with one's choices of main course, salad, dessert, and beverage, then found a table at which to eat. The final price naturally depended upon what one reached for along the way and Manny, for once, reached discretely in deference to his gut. Wouldn't do to have those expensive new pants too tight by the time he got them back to Millwell!

As he got to the end of the line and began looking around for a free table, his eye was caught by someone waving vigorously to get his attention. It was Mr. Gates, the tailor of the men's store where he'd gone looking for conversation and ended up, instead, with a costly purchase. Mr. Gates — who was now enthusiastically beckoning him to share his table.

Manny wished to be invisible but of course that wouldn't happen. He felt he had been treated rather abruptly, if not rudely, by Mr. Gates and could not imagine enjoying a meal in his company. Too polite to yield to such a feeling, he slowly approached the table with an "are you sure?" question on his face.

"Sit down! Sit down!" said Mr. Gates, half-rising from his chair and cordially extending his hand. "Leland Gates, here. I'm surprised you're not dining in Hotel Julian. That's where I'd be if I had the wherewithal."

"Manfred Streeter," said Manny, whose handshake was not vigorous but was sincere, nonetheless. "What a surprise."

His surprise extended when Mr. Gates then said, "Hey, sorry I cut you off this morning. The store manager frowns on the help gossiping with the customers. And you caught me off guard when you asked about the Markay family."

Manny decided to let bygones be bygones, allowing his normal courtesy to show but simultaneously decided against much self-disclosure.

"Understood." he said. "I visit my sister from time to time, on the other side of the state, and there's a woman by the name of Markay living there who is a crack alterations person. Says she's from Dubuque. Don't know why I even agreed to look up her people, so no harm done."

"I know who you're talking about—Madeleine Markay!" was Leland Gates' astonishing answer.

Manny, who was unloading the contents of his tray, nearly dropped it all. "You got me curious," he said, trying for a nonchalant tone.

"The Markay family used to be big in this town" said Mr. Gates.

"I don't know as they ever were as important as they thought they were, but the first arrivals came here from France at least seventy years ago claiming they were from the family of Father Marquette, the Mississippi River explorer. Might be true, might not. Anyway, they had money from someplace. Changed the family name to "Markay," built a mansion to live in and set up a business as pattern makers. Claimed that's what their family had done in France for many generations."

"Patterns makers for what?" Manny asked.

"Clothes, of course," Mr. Gates said "That was a time when stores sold fabric, not ready made garments. The Markay family was pretty prosperous and every generation was expected to learn the business. Madeleine Markay and her brother, Armand, are the only ones left with that name and both were part of the business. But she's not in Dubuque anymore and he has an unlisted home telephone number."

"And what about the business?" asked Manny.

"Well, for sure, it doesn't amount to much these days. Times have changed. He has a few people working for him and I've heard they make patterns for uniforms going to universities and such. Armand does a little work privately, but hard to say who his customers are. They probably pay through the nose for his services. Maybe multimillionaires who have all their clothes handmade."

"Where does Madeleine Markay come in, and how did you get to know her?" was Manny's next query. He knew he was being forward in asking but thought he needed to know.

Leland Gates hesitated a minute, then shrugged. "I got to Dubuque by working my way up the Mississippi from New Orleans when I left the Navy. I was out of money, didn't want to go back to South Dakota, and needed a job. Hired on with the Markay Pattern Company to learn the trade of pattern maker 'cause I'd always been kind of handy with a needle. Sailors would come to me to fix their uniforms after they'd ripped 'em up a little on shore leave.

"Madeleine Markay was at the company at the same time. Of course, I knew better than to try to get chummy with her. She was a beautiful woman and way out of my league. Plus, her brother would have killed me if I'd gotten too close. She was in her early thirties at that time so maybe he'd been chasing guys away from her all her life."

Manny thought he got the picture. "So how did she get out to western Iowa? I'd think she'd have had a better life here, with the family money and reputation."

Silence. Mr. Gates took a few bites of mashed potato and a couple of swallows of water. Embarrassed, Manny looked down at his own plate and ate a forkful or so. He had stepped over some kind of line, he knew, and his dinner companion had maybe said all that he was going to say.

When he finally looked up, Leland Gates wore the expression of a person who had decided to tell all.

"The family always was, from the beginning, faithful to their Catholic beliefs and Dubuque is quite the Catholic town. Lots of stuff going on in that respect. Madeleine belatedly got it in her head that she wanted to join a convent. That really got her brother upset, but the clergy talked him out of it and he had to let her go. Nobody knows what happened after that because in a year or so, here she comes out of the convent, home to brother. She was obviously pregnant, big as a cow, and wouldn't say who got her that way. In a convent! Some said it was a handsome Irishman who hung around doing manual labor for the nuns. Then the whispers really started and the fingers began pointing at Father Sidney.

The Church paid the rumors no heed and Father Sidney got sent to a Catholic enclave out in Denver. That left the Irishman and anytime somebody asked him if he was the guilty party he denied knowing the woman and was ready to back up the denial with his fists. Claimed he was being set up by the parish as a patsy. Eventually, he moved to Moline and out of sight, out of mind."

Manny was uneasy. Pregnant unmarried women were something he knew about. Not personally, oh dear no, but even small towns like Millwell saw their share of them. Each generation, a few girls got pregnant and were hastened into marriage while local women counted on their fingers and smiled knowingly when the subsequent babies were declared to be premature. But the girls didn't end up old and homely, living in abject poverty across the state without family or friends to lighten their days, as Miss Markay had. They lived to have other children, homes and friends.

"What about the baby?" he asked.

"Nobody ever knew," said Mr. Gates. "I heard rumors it was adopted out by the nuns and I suppose that's what happened although there were other, really awful rumors that it had mysteriously disappeared before it was a week old. and I don't know what they were based on. Armand sure wouldn't have allowed a little Markay bastard hanging around in Dubuque and would have done whatever was necessary to make sure of that. Anyway, before too long the talk was that he'd sent his sister Madeleine away to live in what you might call 'exile.'"

Manny thought of one more question. "Did this Armand always live such an exemplary life?"

"Hell, no," said Mr. Gates. "He never had what you'd call girl friends, and he never got married, but he took bad advantage of every young woman hired at the pattern works. Madeleine had a friend, Neva Casey, who was smart enough to be a secretary, and he led her on something awful and then, every time it looked like he might seriously court her, he'd start ignoring her and play up to somebody else. Not so long ago, I heard a rumor that she's still hanging around the pattern company and letting him bully her."

That ended the discussion of the Markay family, as Manny could plainly perceive. Leland Gates had the facial expression of a person who knows he's talked too much and Manny wished he could reassure him that nothing said would go farther. The two of them made some polite talk about the war and how the Allies were doing and then Manny excused himself from the table. "Long day tomorrow, so I'd better be getting back to the hotel. Sure has been nice making your acquaintance."

"Well, say 'hello' to Madeleine for me," said Mr. Gates. "She probably doesn't remember me but she might. I sure spent enough time staring at her when we were both working at the pattern company. She never let on she knew, but I could tell by the way she'd smile into thin air and toss her hair that she knew that she was being admired. Just tell her you met a little old guy with an anchor tattoo who'd thought she was really something."

Manny shook hands with Mr. Gates and went back to the hotel. He suspected that Leland Gates was a lonely man with a modest income from doing clothing alterations and who was without close family. He did not identify with him since he, himself, had a good and steady job, pleasant rooms over the Millwell post office, a certain amount of money in savings, and identity and respect in a nice little western Iowa town. He was not a bit like Leland Gates. Not a bit.

The next morning, Manny got the Chevrolet out again and went looking for the Markay pattern works. It was most surely not in the part of town where commercial buildings stood, nor was it anywhere in the heart of the city. When he finally found it, he thought, "Well sure. I might have known."

An ambitiously built Italianate-style house of immense proportions stood on the very edge of the oldest part of the historic district. A discreet sign identified it as one of the earliest Dubuque homes and business locations. In ornate letters, "Patterns by Markay" celebrated its past and present glories.

Going strictly by instinct, Manny decided to approach the front entrance. He was nervous, not totally in contact with his intent, and no longer felt an urge to communicate Miss Markay's demise to possible relatives of hers. On some level, that may never have been his true intent and, since his conversation with Leland Gates, he had begun to admit it to himself. When he thought about the description of Madeleine's brother Armand, the images created a direct pipeline to his bladder. But never mind—he was not a coward. He would lift the heavy knocker on the front door and force it up and down as long as it took to gain entrance.

That he was spared. A neat notice on the door said to enter and so he did. A reserved looking woman who had passed her salad days was sitting at a desk in the central hall doing some kind of paper work. She looked up as Manny entered and, when he had thoroughly closed the door and taken the steps necessary to approach her desk, looked at him enquiringly. He would have to be the one to speak.

"I have heard," he began. Then he began again, amending his words to "Somebody told me," then tried a third time. "It has come to my attention that the Markay Pattern Company can help me."

The chilly lady acquired a more genial look. "Are you by chance from Stanford University? We understood you were coming next week."

"No, I'm afraid not," he reluctantly admitted. "I am under the impression that this firm also does work for individuals?" It came out as a question, which of course was asking for contempt. However—and surprisingly — the receptionist maintained a tolerant mode.

"Certainly," she said. "That, however, is to be discussed

personally with Mr. Armand Markay. I will inform him that you are here. Your name, please?"

Manny gulped. He wanted to come up with a fictitious name but couldn't think of one. "Manfred Streeter," he said, with as much stateliness as he could master. He was in for it now.

The receptionist disappeared to an inner room and when she returned she wasn't alone. Accompanying her was a tall, thin man who looked to be in his early seventies and whose bearing gave the impression that he daily dined on small town postmasters. The receptionist looked uneasy, even a little scared. Perhaps she should have gotten rid of such a dubious customer and would later pay for her inefficiency?

Nevertheless, the man now smiled and Manny thought he had never seen such perfect teeth. He recalled Doc's admiration of Madeleine Markay's teeth and thought Doc should see this set of choppers. "Must run in the Markay family," was his irrelevant reflection.

"Thank you, Miss Casey," said the man in a frigid tone.

The receptionist blanched.

"Mr. Streeter," crooned Armand Markay, "please step into my office." He led the way into his private space, which Manny guessed had been the chief drawing room in a bygone era. It was huge and gorgeously furnished with an immense desk that looked fit to be the administrative center for presidents and kings. Carved flourishes extended across its width and down its regal dimensions. Armand Markay took his rightful place behind it, gesturing toward a sumptuous easy chair that Manny understood he was to occupy. He did so, taking care to sit very straight as if under the observation of a mighty overseer.

"Let me guess," said Mr. Markay. "You are perhaps a writer? They often are—uh—rather reticent people."

At Manny's puzzled look, he quickly amended his guess. "Perhaps an actor? Many of your fellow thespians have come to Markay Patterns for wardrobe assistance."

He gestured toward a cluster of photographs on the wall and Manny recognized the visages of Gene Autry, Lionel Barrymore, Lou Costello.

Lard asses, all, thought Manny. They could use design help with their pants!

The other actors were people from before his time.

Manny shook his head ever so slightly. Under the circumstances, he couldn't exactly admit to being a small town postmaster, could he? "Ah, well, ah, I'm in government," he said.

Armand Markay looked ever so slightly relieved to at last have a pigeonhole for Manny.

"Well!" he said. "We have worked with several people in government." He nodded toward a portrait of the current president. "If one is, perhaps, a bit disabled, one's trousers must conceal a great deal!"

Manny felt as if he now knew more than he had any right to know. What could he say to cover his vulnerability?

No problem, since conversation by him was not presently needed. His host proceeded to deliver an oration of some length, all to the point that Markay Patterns—and he, specifically—could design patterns and garments that would solve the sartorial problems of every man of note, worldwide, regardless of his figure flaws.

The people in Millwell had a term for such people, Manny thought. In Millwell's vernacular, people like Armand Markay would be described as "stuck on themselves." To be stuck on oneself was, in Millwell, an appalling trait. To a person, small town people had no use for those who claimed any kind of superiority. Their children might grow up to discuss concepts like "self-confidence" but those terms would not be understood by their earlier forbears.

Evidently, if one came from an illustrious family in Dubuque, one could go ahead and be as self-assured as one wished but Manny watched with concealed disapproval as his host pointed to easels displaying artistic sketches of coats and trousers, each feature explained in beautiful penmanship.

It was penmanship that Manny recognized. Now shown in generous size on the displays, he had seen it before on the address side of a penny postcard addressed to Madeleine Markay. He watched with fascination as Armand Markay's graceful long hands gestured and pointed with a silver pen that was undoubtedly sterling, in a rhythm consistent with his bragging.

Hands, Manny saw, that were of a size and strength to successfully wrap around the neck of a reclusive seamstress. Or that of a newborn.

Or, perhaps, that of a receptionist who knew too much?

What should he now say and do? Manny was frightened and his bladder tightened. If he gave his name and told where he lived, would he experience those skilled and frightening hands around his own neck? His original ambition to confront Miss Markay's brother turned to mush.

Afterward, he never knew from whence had come the inspiration that got him off the hook. What he did was rise, slowly, from his comfortable chair and say, as if with great reluctance, "Personally, I wish I could afford your services." Here, he gave a small laugh of self-deprecation. Then, the brilliant stroke. "I will report your abilities to Mr. Hoover, who will be most appreciative."

J. Edgar! A well-known and terrifying lard ass!

Armand Markay blanched ever so slightly, then recovered. Did he think the F.B.I. was on his trail for murder? Or was he, in the long run, sufficiently stuck on himself to believe the omnipotent Hoover had heard of him and was interested in his pattern making skills? He would never know because, contrary to his extensive business instincts, this time he would not investigate. This Manfred Streeter could make his report, whatever it was, but if Hoover was interested in a well-fitting pair of pants, Hoover would have to come to him personally.

Manny was accompanied to the door by a subdued Armand Markay and bade farewell with good wishes that reeked of insincerity. Stepping outside, Manny turned slightly before the door closed behind him and looked backward just in time to see Neva Casey, the receptionist, trying to control a look of pain as Armand Markay grasped her shoulder and twisted.

Why, after all these years, was she still there submitting to intermittent abuse? Manny knew the answer to that one, courtesy of his years in the Millwell post office as recipient of town gossip. Men who bullied had a pattern. When their women threatened to leave them, they would frequently pretend a great abiding love—a facade they maintained until their women decided they were now going to be treated better and had once again settled down. When that part of the cycle occurred, the bully would resume his old behavior and when the woman was next seen in public she would be a mass of bruises. Except for the cases, rare but not all that rare, when the man ended up killing her.

Manny walked to his car with shivers running down his spine, totally convinced that when Armand Markay no longer needed Miss Casey, who certainly knew too much about him, he would do away with her.

Climbing into his Chevy, Manny reflected upon the practicality of getting his personal belongings from the hotel and driving back to Millwell that very afternoon. He had come to Dubuque seeking information about Madeleine Markay, he had found it, and there was absolutely nothing he could do to cancel the inevitable.

When he got back to the hotel and had parked the car, Manny sat in it for a long time, thinking and thinking. Was he truly as incompetent as he feared? Was he going to let this situation go without lifting a finger to stop it? It was too late to help Miss Markay, the hapless seamstress who had lived and died in Millwell, but was there nothing to motivate her brother, Armand, to spare Neva Casey?

Instead of going to his hotel room, perhaps stopping to eat lunch, Manny walked down the street to the handsome Dubuque post office, went up to one of its service windows, and laid down a nickel in exchange for several postcards. On his way out of the building he paused for a moment before large murals that depicted an Indian village, steamboats and early settlers. A little Grant Woodish in style, he mused, then decided that any post office deemed worthy of murals was nothing to criticize.

He made another stop, one that took him into a Woolworth's, where he purchased a bottle of blue ink and an inexpensive fountain pen. Forgoing lunch, he sat at the desk in his hotel room, filled the pen with medium blue ink, and—with an eye on the copy he had made of Miss Markay's note to Shirley—he practiced writing on one of the postcards.

Despite your efforts, I have returned to Dubuque and will remain here.

Your soul is in mortal danger and you will be punished if you do not repent.

Two practice postcards to get the message properly fitted into the space, then a final one that looked as authentic as if Miss

Markay, herself, had written it.

He signed it "M," then wrote a second card.

***You are being watched by me, by all the saints, and by the
devil. It will soon be too late if you do not forego evil.***

He signed that one with an "M" as well, then left his hotel room
to walk to the post office once more. His feet hurt but the pain was
lightened by hope as he dropped the first card he'd written into the
slot for outgoing mail. It was still early enough in the afternoon to
assure it of local delivery the next day. One more nap, one more
dinner in the dining room,, would be his reward for a task well
accomplished. He would have the chicken this time and investigate
the properties of the 'flan' that was listed as a choice of dessert.

The next morning, blessedly free of a stomach ache, he paid his
hotel bill and went over to the men's shop to pick up his new
trousers. Relieved that Leland Gates was not yet on the premises, he
told the shop manager that he didn't have the time for a second
fitting—to just give him the pants. Leaving Dubuque, he swung past
the post office and mailed the second of the postcards he had
written. If Armand Markay got postcards two days running, both
from a sister that he had to know for sure was dead, fear would
surely cause him to stop whatever he had planned with regard to his
pitiable receptionist. In a few years he would be aged and his
business would dissolve around him. Patterns by Markay would
belong to past history and nobody would miss it—except, perhaps,
a few people who had plenty of money but not enough of it to avoid
having rear ends out of proportion to the rest of their anatomies.

Madeleine Markay would be as dead as ever but, Manny
thought, deserved to have her full name, at least. He would—
anonymously, of course—cause a small monument to be placed on
her pauper's grave in the corner of the Millwell town cemetery.
People would come into the post office and stop at his window to
tell him about it and he would feign surprise. When Doc would
remark, as he inevitably would, "I told you she was a patrician!
Ordinary folks don't have teeth like that. Madeleine is a name for a
genuine lady!" he would assume an inscrutable expression—as any
of J. Edgar Hoover's agents worth his salt would surely do.

87

A month after his visit to Dubuque, Manny could no longer stand not knowing if there had been any visible outcome to his postcards and thought he could probably get by with calling Leland Gates on the pretext of thanking him for a good alterations outcome.

Knowing that any phone call he made from Millwell would be listened to by Shirley Spence, he took an afternoon off one Wednesday when Myrtle Schaefer was at the post office window and went over to Denison. Locating the town's telephone office, he placed a call to the men's store in Dubuque where he had bought his pants and asked for Leland Gates.

Mr. Gates was surprised and pleased, especially when Manny told him that he realized he'd never had a chance to thank him for a superb alteration job.

"Well, that's nice of you," said Mr. Gates. "Come back any time. Plenty more pants where those came from! By the way, how's Madeleine Markay?"

"Oh, dear," said Manny. "I'm afraid she has passed away. She will be missed."

"That's too bad," said Leland Gates. "I wonder if that's what made her brother Armand so upset that he signed that fancy old house over to the Church to use as a home for unwed mothers. Then he left town without, as far as anybody knows, leaving a forwarding address. Neva Casey says he talked about moving to Quebec and going into a monastery."

Manny had to suppress a gasp of relief. "How is Miss Casey," he asked.

"Pretty happy," said Mr. Gates. "Evidently Armand offered her retirement with a huge sum of money attached and she's having the time of her life, joining all kinds of clubs and helping out at the Red Cross."

Manny said goodbye to Leland Gates with a promise to stop by Dubuque sometime when he was in the area. He didn't think that was likely to happen but one never knew what would come up in the future.

Then he chortled. "Made a difference," he said to the rear view mirror as he started the drive back to Millwell. Neva Casey rolling bandages at the Red Cross was a much better outcome than death at Armand Markay's lethal hands. The U. S. Postal Service had its rules, of course — and he had disregarded a few of them — but it just didn't understand the situations that a small town postmaster sometimes had to face.

Dene Hellman

WAREHOUSE ANNIVERSARY

I'M NOT SUPPOSED TO INTERACT with the customers. This is an upscale warehouse, whatever "upscale" means, and our customers devote a lot of attention to what they're buying. Everything is in such big packages that a purchase is more of an investment than a casual checking off of a shopping list. People usually come alone or with one other person: they look at things and make decisions like they are buying shares in the stock market. No hand-to-mouth customers in our warehouse!

All the employees below management level are called "colleagues" and there are those who say it's just another word for "flunkies." I'm not given to being sarcastic like that. A job is a job. Our responsibilities are to keep the shelves stocked, know the layout of the whole product floor and the pedigree of the items on the shelves that we tend. Customers can see us hanging around if they really want some help. We are trained to respond with very polite, no-pressure voices.

The customers who are thinking about a television set or a printer may want a little assistance but the ones who come to my department don't come up with a lot of questions. Not many impulse items are on display—just stuff that buyers have already researched as much as needed.

All of them are after price, that's all.

The pet owners know they need flea medicine, they just don't know if they should pop for the expensive kind. It's a matter of how much money they have, how many pets, and how much they believe the hype about brands.

The folks who need a new clothes washer or dryer have already looked in stores at the mall and at appliance shops. What they have to decide is if our somewhat lower price is going to get them the exact same features as the machine they fell for at Sears.

Then there are the mattresses. These days, there are dozens of different pedigrees for mattresses. Firm, plush, pillow-top, stuff that lets one person in a bed choose to have something different from the other person in the bed, and so on. In our warehouse the mattresses

90

are all the way to the far wall. They don't make a very interesting display, standing up on end the way they do, but folks are usually looking at something they already know about. For one thing, they know they can trust us and they're not so sure about all those places that advertise too good to be true prices, just because it's Labor Day or something. Then, too, the articles in consumer magazines rate us pretty high so if a lady says she's tired of pawing through our merchandise and wants to go to a place that just sells mattresses, her husband is apt to lay a guilt trip on her and tell her she needs to understand the advantages of buying from us.

I like to be of help but I have to say what the managers tell me because I don't actually have much first-hand knowledge about most of this stuff. The warehouse managers are always referring to "consumers," using the term interchangeably with "customers." To tell the truth, I'm not much of a consumer or customer, either. My wife, Marlene, takes care of the laundry; we don't have any pets, and I don't know from one end of the month to the other how much money we have in the bank. She does all of that, which is appropriate considering that her job teaching school brings in quite a bit more than what I make at the warehouse.

Personally, I think we are a little better off than she lets on. We could have a regular house with a garage and room to grown some vegetables but she decided on our town home because it is fancier than any house we can afford and also because taking care of it is easier than a house would be.

Having a dog is something I've wanted ever since I got out of the army but Marlene says, "Who'd walk him? I'm in school all day and you work eight to twelve hour shifts." That's true; it wouldn't be fair to a dog, especially a good-sized one, to be inside all the time and not get any exercise.

I tried to sell her on one of those big flat television screens we display in the front of the store but Marlene doesn't watch television hardly at all. "We don't need one," she says. "I have papers to grade in the evening and whenever you lay back in your recliner to watch a program you just end up going to sleep."

She's right but there isn't a lot to stay awake for at our house.

"You should see these pillow top mattresses," I said to Marlene, getting back to the subject of our warehouse. "They're a whole lot different from all the ones I've ever slept on. They look so

comfortable that I want to lay down on one whenever I'm tired."
"Your back okay?" asks Marlene.
"Yeah, as far as I know," I answer.
"Then we still have a few years with the mattress we have," says Marlene.

Marlene has about another ten years to go until retirement and she probably worries that if we give in to every fancy new thing that comes along we'll have some hard years ahead of us. I wouldn't say she's tight but she sure is frugal. She gets a new car every five years and I get the old one. That works okay; I drive to work and back, that's about all, and if we go someplace together—like her mother's house—we take her car.

Every summer she goes on vacation for about ten days with some of her girlfriends and that's fine with me. I don't like to go to strange places very much and I take my own vacation during the week she's gone. With the two weekends included, that is one glorious time. I watch whatever is on the tube and eat whatever I want and go over to one of the local bars a few times to have a couple of beers and watch sports on the great big television set they have.

When I got out of the Army, after the Gulf War, I was lucky and didn't have any disabilities but I just didn't have any urge to go to school or learn a trade. That didn't set too well with Marlene.

We had gotten married before I went in and she always counted on us having a good double income someday.

But I went to clerking in stores after getting out of the service and wasn't embarrassed about it. My dad had been behind the counter in a hardware store all his life and our family thought that was fine. We didn't have a lot of fancy stuff at home but we had enough to eat and wear and us kids knew we needed to have a paper route or something if we wanted any spending money. When did work like my dad's get to be classified as minimum wage and lose its honor? My folks were married for fifty-two years and seemed to be contented with the circumstances of their lives; my dad held his head up with pride wherever he went.

Marlene told me a couple of weeks ago that we, ourselves, are coming up on our twenty-fifth anniversary and she has picked out where we should go eat by way of celebration. Oh boy was I surprised! She named this fancy restaurant on the edge of town that only gives you a choice between two different items. You got no control over the price and once you've chosen they pick out everything else you should eat. Every course they put down has a wine alongside that is supposed to be the right thing. Then you get shocked with the price they charge and that means a huge tip goes along with it and then the head waiter bows and says something to you in French and tells somebody else to go get your car for you. Marlene wants to go there so bad that she has taken to coaching me about how I should act and that is how I know all this. I don't think she is counting on a real good time but she wants to share our experience with her friends later in the week.

I hope she's not expecting anything else from me that would be worth "sharing." As a rule, she is opposed to getting friendly after the lights are out. It's hard to tell, though, what all she thinks is appropriate for an anniversary.

It figures that I'm supposed to come up with a nice anniversary present—which is okay by me but Marlene has all the know-how about our money so what do I do? For the last year she has mentioned jewelry every time she had an excuse. "You should see Valerie's diamond birthstone ring!" she'll say, or refer to one of the women she teaches with who also got lucky on her birthday. "Mavis got this fabulous diamond necklace from her husband," she told me. Actually, she told me several times.

Mavis's husband is a dermatologist, I know, so the diamond necklace wasn't any skin off his nose. However, I get the idea that Marlene would like some kind of diamond that she can brag about to her friends. The trouble is, I don't know how much money we have or even if Marlene would, in all honesty, want me to spend any of it on something that isn't even practical.

I took it up with Cressie, the girl who folds and refolds the clothes on the apparel tables. She doesn't give any advice to customers—that's not her job—but she has to watch helplessly while they unfold and hold up every pair of jeans and sweater and tee shirt that's displayed so they can guess at the right fit. When they leave to go look at something else, she has to go over and refold and restack every single thing. She is a pleasant, patient person, though, and that makes her nice to talk to. I told her that I suspected Marlene of hinting for some kind of diamond jewelry.

"Whatever that stuff costs," I said, "I don't know if Marlene wants me to get it. She always seems picky about her stuff and brags when she gets something nice on sale. It's just possible that she'd be really mad at me if I went overboard with a gift."

"Would you like me to check out the diamond jewelry in the upfront showcase?" Cressie asks me, and I'm relieved.

"You do that," I say. "I'd feel like a fool up there handling that stuff."

Cressie hunted me up a couple of hours later and said, "I don't know, Frank. You can't really get anything special for less than a couple of thousand dollars, even though our prices here in the warehouse are cheaper than if you went to an uptown jewelry store."

Right away, I knew Marlene would be pretty mad if I spent a lot of money like that. What to do instead? The next chance I got, I expressed myself to Millicent. Millicent is the food demonstrator in the bakery department, a nice little person who is too much on the elderly side to be on her feet all day handing out little paper cups with pieces of strudel or cinnamon rolls. I looked for a lull in her work and it took a while to happen. She is always surrounded by customers who act starved for a taste of warehouse pastry and it's a wonder she has time to go to the ladies' room once in a while.

Butting in when there was, finally, some space between customers, I laid the question out as to whether she thought I should get my wife diamond jewelry for our anniversary or if she thought I'd get in trouble for spending that much money on an impractical gift.

Millicent was cutting a strudel up into little pieces that had to be just enough and not too much and she looked worried about maybe giving me the wrong answer. "You know what, Frank," she said. "It's the thought that counts, not the gift!"

I'd heard that one before and didn't know if it would apply to Marlene but told her she was probably right. Thanking her, I headed back toward my department.

All of this wasn't getting me any closer to an anniversary present and if I knew what was good for me I'd have one in hand in a few days. I started spending my lunch time looking all around the warehouse for something suitable. The grocery merchandise was out. I thought a little bit about getting one of those fancy decorated cakes in the bakery refrigerator.

Millicent saw me looking and started nodding her head up and down.

"Great idea," she said. "The decorator folks will make you an especially elegant one, seeing as it's you who's buying!"

"Nah," I said. "Marlene is always on a diet and would probably crown me if I brought home something chock full of calories."

Then I looked at the clothes displays a little while but Cressie caught me at it. "Don't even think it," she said. "None of this stuff is anniversary worthy. Keep looking. You maybe should still consider getting something from the jewelry case."

Marlene and I had already been through discussions about television sets and mattresses, so that was out. That left the garden department and I wandered up and down the places where the display was arranged. The outdoor furniture was pretty nice but we didn't have any outdoors to put it in. Same for the grills.

Then, by golly, I saw it! It was right in the middle of the solar light display—and said, "Special! Special!" to me. It was a solar-lit owl that stood at least three feet tall and it was just as cute as the dickens. The garden department colleague had rigged it up to something electrical that made it look the way it would outside at night, when it had all day to soak up sunshine. That owl was all colors glowing away together: red and blue and green, and it had this crest on top of its head that shone in bright gold. We don't have a yard, but there would sure be enough room in our little 10 x 10 patch of grass to set it up. Considering that it was purely ornamental, it cost quite a bit—but I had a few dollars in my wallet so I bought it on the spot. When I showed it to Cressie she gave me a funny look and tried again with the jewelry.

"Maybe we should give the diamonds another look," she said.

"I just can't believe Marlene would want me to spend that much money," says I.

"Okay," Cressie says, looking more resigned. "If you'll trust me with the owl, I'll take it home and gift wrap it just specially for your anniversary."

"Sure," I said. "I wouldn't be any good at that but you're right. Marlene would likely appreciate a nice looking package."

On Thursday, the Big Day, Sandra, a colleague that looks after the fresh flower display, stopped me when I walked past her station. "Hey," she said, grabbing me by the arm. "Millicent told me that I can't let you go home without at least three bouquets of fresh red roses all put together!"

I shook my head. "Sorry. Marlene favors artificial flowers. She thinks she may have some allergies and, besides, she doesn't like fussing with stuff."

Millicent and Cressie were standing over at one side and I saw them and Sandra exchange that kind of desperate look they'd all taken to giving me.

Cressie had the wrapped-up owl waiting for me when we went out to the parking lot after our shift. It was the nicest looking package I'd ever seen, with special "Happy Anniversary" paper and a big fluffy bow that had silvery streamers hanging down from it.

Marlene was really going to have something to "share" with her friends, I thought, as I settled that pretty owl package into the back seat and drove home.

A HOUSE FOR HER

HOLDING HIS BREATH, he watches as they lay out the boundary lines. He knows they would prefer that he stay away, at least until that part is done and the first studs are in place — but he is incapable of disregarding the opening moves in the most important thing he has done in a long while.

It came to him one day when he saw carpenters put an addition on a building in his neighborhood: he should build a house for *her*. He, personally, is contented with apartment living. Moreover, he is such an anti-materialist that he owns only two or three water glasses, forks, spoons and knives. He has one towel and one set of sheets. Nevertheless, he guesses that women want to have their own bit of real-estate and prefer furnishings to cover all kinds of circumstances. His mother was like that and probably still is; her expensive senior living apartment, for which he pays, is likely stuffed with unnecessary luxury goods. He doesn't go there anymore, weary of her advice and criticism.

In a rare conversation with a fellow worker, he asks how one goes about starting from scratch to build a house. He phrases himself obliquely but the associate catches on right away and tells him to find a piece of land, then look for a house plan, then choose a construction company and get financing from a bank.

"My wife and I lucked out big time," the fellow worker says. "I wasn't crazy at first about the cost of all those frills. I mean, what did we need with hand-made Mexican tile in the family room and a kitchen stove suitable for a four-star chef? But my wife was set on having the best and our house value has doubled in just a few years!"

He doesn't think his associate made the right choice in going for so many frills, but he supposes the guy's wife didn't take the environment into consideration. A lot of people don't.

He is lucky with finding a building lot. On his way home from the office one day, he drives through a pleasant neighborhood and observes a "For Sale" sign on a vacant piece of ground. Seeing no advantage in being secretive, he knocks on a door or two and finds the lot belongs to a family that has held it for a long time. They are tired of mowing the vegetation that persists in springing up on the vacant land, their kids have grown up and don't need it for ball games, and they are ready to cash in on their initial investment. They ask for a lot of money while pointing out the advantages of living in an established neighborhood. He does not argue the price and immediately writes a check. His co-worker tells him the next day that he was pretty rash in purchasing in an old neighborhood but that he now needs to register the deed. A lawyer is suggested.

The very next weekend he takes the time to go to a large place that sells things to carpenters and to people who like to do their own home projects. He goes through literature racks to find house plan books and marvels that so many kinds of houses have been designed. He can only guess what kind of a house she would like, but this is to be a surprise so he will have to buy several plan books and then choose from among them according to his best guess. The lot isn't huge so there will be limitations but, after all, if he opts for a top quality home in an environmentally appropriate size, he will surely succeed in pleasing her.

One thing he knows: unlike his fellow worker, he doesn't want one of the behemoths like those being built in new places on the edge of the city. To him, many of those are monsters of ridiculous design that must inevitably and indecently eat up electricity and other resources. Of course, this house will have solar panels.

He studies the house plan books and, with great difficulty, tries to imagine himself going from room to room. His personal lifestyle requires little beyond a place to use his computer, a place to eat, a simple bedroom with closet space for the clothing required at work, and a small bathroom where he can shower and shave. If necessary, he could accommodate all those needs in one room. These house plans not only allow for those activities but allow for the additional needs and wants that *she* will have: they seem so much like overkill that he has moments of doubt about the entire project.

However, one plan book seems better to him than the others. It is titled Small Prestige Homes and the dimensions of its various homes look appropriate for the lot he has purchased. Each house has costly amenities that, once built, will add quality to the structure. There are many sky lights and conservatories that will allow plants to flourish even in the winter.

He makes a choice, sends for the plans, and has no misgivings, going forward; he has made the correct decision.

His associate at work tells him that he will now have to get bids from contractors and go to a bank to get financing, but he can simplify all that. He asks which local contractor is the best, puts the plans on that builder's desk, and accepts the estimate he is given with thanks. From there, he goes to his accountant, whose advice he relied on when buying his mother's assisted living apartment, and who decides at all times what he should do with his money.

He has a lot of money, certainly. After developing a computer program that everyone wants, he gets endless royalties. Having no use for money, beyond modest sums for his daily food, shelter and transportation, he allows the accountant to take all the funds that remain and invest them as he sees fit to do. Every three months he is shown balance sheets that say he has quite a lot more money than he had three months before.

The accountant seems pleased that some of those funds will now go into building a house and, asking too many personal questions about the woman for whom it is being done, says, "About time!" That causes a certain amount of discomfort. He knows he is blushing and being more reticent than he needs to be, but that is just who he is—a very private individual.

The builder is undoubtedly relieved that he isn't there watching the preparations. He wants to, but part of his job is traveling a good part of the continent and some of Europe on behalf of his computer innovations. This is tiresome; he would rather be home than having to make endless technical explanations. Worse than the explanations are the necessary refusals of offers for dinner and other amusements. He knows they all have a label that they pin on him, perhaps correctly, but he is who he is.

When he gets home from his trip, the first thing he does is drive to the place where the house is being built; he inhales so sharply that it startles him. Instead of the skeleton, the whole building has been covered with sheathing. A couple of workmen are still there, even though it is early evening. They are cleaning things up for the commencement of work tomorrow morning, recognize him from former sightings, and don't deny him the privilege of walking through the rooms. He can only guess what is what, except for the bathrooms that have huge tub and shower components already set in.

He has some time before he has to go on another business trip so it is a rare day when he doesn't go to the embryo house to see how it is doing. Some of the people who work there haven't met him and are quite irritated when he asks about the function of the pipes and wires and panels. Humbly, he begs their pardon and assures them that he isn't contradicting their expertise.

The general contractor catches up with him one day and begins to ask bewildering questions that have to do with styles and colors and windows. When he can't come up with coherent answers, the builder says he has a semi-solution.

"A lot of us guys aren't real savvy about that stuff," he says, soothingly. "If I can make a suggestion, there is a lady who calls herself a decorator and from what I've seen of the places she has designed, she is pretty good at it. Usually, she works for companies that are putting up spec houses and makes good use of the budget they give her. In your case, you have a more liberal purse and I'll bet she would do a great job pleasing you and (pause) your Mrs. or intended or whoever is the lady in your life."

He isn't quite sure what to do and asks his accountant, who laughs and says, "Well, it isn't that you have to do any penny pinching. Sure! Go ahead! Get the decorator woman involved. At least she'll have had some experience with making choices and if you don't like what she comes up with, you can pay somebody else to do it over."

At last, the house is finished and the decorator has, with his agreement, hired a landscaper. Knowing nothing about gardens except that grass lawns must continuously be mowed and are very wasteful, he explains this to the decorator. The landscaper is then given carte blanche to create a beautiful garden where things can be grown for both usefulness and beauty, but will not require constant attack with a machine. There is a pergola for grape vines and a cozy barbecue pit for entertaining. A bird sanctuary is set apart from the rest of the garden, promising privacy and peace for feathered visitors. A space for vegetable gardening is ready to be planted in the springtime. He hopes *she* will enjoy all of this.

The builder finally announces that it's time for something called a "walk- through" wherein it is mutually agreed that everything is as it should be. With a degree of helplessness, he asks his colleague at work and his accountant if they will make the walk with him. Both ask if they may bring their wives, but he refuses because he doesn't think other women should be allowed to see the house before *she* does.

The builder seems to be proud and the decorator has taken many photos, asking if she may use them to secure business from potential clients. At his request, she makes a set for him. During the walk-through, the accountant and the colleague are full of praise. "A little gem!" the accountant says. The colleague says he personally prefers a larger home for his own family, but would just love to have a lot of the cost-saving features that this house represents. Then, he adds, "And wow! What a bachelor pad!" He pokes his elbow into the accountant's arm.

It is time.

Armed with the photos taken by the decorator, he approaches the reception area of his company. *She* is sitting in her usual spot and looks up when he enters. Tossing her long, blonde hair aside, she smiles a warm welcome at him. He walks toward her, his arm outstretched to offer the photos.

"I have built you a house!" he says.

"You have what?" she asks.

"I have built you a house and these photos show how it looks now that it's done! I did everything the way I thought you would like it. Now we just have to move in," he explains.

"You're crazy!" she says and recoils from his hand holding the photos.

"Please," he begs. "Please look at these!" He moves toward her and touches her shoulder.

"You crazy freak," she screams. "Don't you touch me! I'm calling Security!"

The security people arrive within seconds and so does the department manager. "What's going on?" they all want to know.

He tries to explain that he has built a house for her and she begins to cry, moving as far away from him as she can get.

The security people ask him what he has done and why. He answers, totally bewildered, that he's done nothing but try to show her pictures of the house he has built for her.

The department manager asks, gently, "What made you think

she would want you to do that?"

He explains that she has always been so welcoming whenever he enters the department where she is the receptionist, he is certain she is interested in him.

"That's my job!" the woman says. "I'm *supposed* to be cordial to people! Nobody else gets the wrong idea!"

The security people look helplessly at the department manager, who knows he has a very delicate situation on his hands.

"You need to calm down," the manager says to the young woman "He was simply trying to please you and I'm sure we can work this out. Take the rest of the day off and come by to see me tomorrow morning. We'll set up something to your advantage."

To the bewildered security people who know that, somehow, the correct protocol is being evaded, he says, "Just a misunderstanding, folks. You do your jobs very well and I'll personally see to it there's a little extra in your pay envelopes this month."

To *him*, who is standing at one side, still clutching the photos of the house, he says, "I'm sorry you had to go through this. You know these women: they light up for every man they see, then act all insulted when one of us takes them seriously. I know you're disappointed, but there's plenty more fish in the sea."

He knows the entire company will hear the story before the week is out and is so embarrassed that he volunteers for a long trip to Asia that he would ordinarily try to sidestep. She is gone, and he doesn't know if she resigned or was fired. He feels an unaccountable loneliness and is grateful when his colleague invites him to have coffee.

"Tough going," his friend says. "The only difference between you and the rest of us is that you were honorable about your feelings and built her a house."

His accountant tells him, "You know, you have a beautiful little home there. You should move in and enjoy it. I think we can find a housekeeper to keep things up for you."

He says he will think about it and perhaps he will do just that but he isn't ready to make a decision of any kind. He will take his time on his trip to Asia and think about possibilities.

The builder and the decorator woman have offered to look after the house for a couple of months, in his absence, if he will let them show it on a forthcoming Parade of Homes as an advertisement for their talents. That strikes him as a very practical, if temporary, solution. He has made some mistakes, but so have others.

He is pretty sure that *she* will change her mind.

HARE TODAY

IT WAS OBVIOUS WHEN they moved the rabbit that it would cause trauma of some kind.

The rabbit certainly was traumatized, but that was just the beginning of a most unfortunate situation. Doris said they had to do it because a friend of hers, the person who had initially housed the rabbit for the entertainment of her grandkids, was moving out of town to a place that allowed absolutely no pets of any kind. In her "I can solve everything" voice, Doris said that was just fine and to leave everything to her. She knew the local children's museum was setting up an Alice in Wonderland room and a resident white rabbit would be just the thing to have.

Sylvia, who lived down the corridor from Doris in Garden Acres Independent Living, was not so sure it sounded like a practical solution but Doris needed Sylvia to use her minivan to transport the rabbit and emphasized what an all around good deed would be accomplished. Doris had a car of her own but she said it was much too small to hold a cage, an animal, and bags of food. It was perfectly logical, then, that Doris asked Sylvia to help out. What are friends for?

The two women were approximately the same age—in their early seventies—and both enjoyed reasonably good health. Doris was better educated and had retired at age 65 from her job running the local library. Sylvia had more money than Doris even though the job she held for many years was as a checkout person at the local Food Shoppe. She hadn't received much in the way of wages but one day a man who brokered frozen vegetables and entrees came in for a conference with the store manager, liked Sylvia's looks, and asked her out to dinner. Before she knew it, she found herself married to him and the two of them then enjoyed twenty-three years of domestic happiness before he keeled over with a fatal heart attack.

He left her the sole recipient of his considerable estate and thus able to pay the fee for residency at Garden Delight, with plenty of income left over in case she wanted to travel or take up elaborate forms of philanthropy.

She was, however, in awe of Doris because of what she assumed was Doris's superior intellect, as well as her experience with supervising a staff. Sylvia's husband made all their decisions while he was alive and Sylvia was glad to allow him to do so, never complaining that he was authoritarian. Perhaps she was, therefore, a logical person to be Doris's friend.

For her part, Doris was certainly glad to find a generous associate like Sylvia whom she could benefit with her leadership qualities.

Wrestling the rabbit cage into Sylvia's van was difficult. The rear space was large enough to accommodate it, but not by a lot. All the bags of food were loaded onto the passenger seats.

Doris led the way to the children's museum, driving just the tiniest bit over the speed limit, and when Sylvia accelerated to keep up, the cage in the rear began sliding around. Sylvia was frightened for the rabbit because if the cage tipped, so would its occupant. She empathized with all her heart and, when they arrived at the museum, discovered that, yes, the rabbit had suffered a terrible journey and was shaking. Sylvia longed to hold it in her arms to calm its fears but Doris said it would be impractical to take it out of its confinement. Someone in the museum would come out and carry both cage and rabbit into its future location, where it would settle down in no time, she said.

The two women had differing views about the museum. Doris knew some of the women behind its origin and upkeep and had the utmost regard for them. Actually, some of the women had been on the library board when she was head honcho there and for the most part had backed whatever ideas she had put forth.

Sylvia didn't know any of the museum board, except as Food Shoppe customers, and hoped they were nicer to children than they had been to her when she rang up their food prices. Of course, that was before her marriage; nowadays, they didn't even recognize her as a prior grocery store cashier and instead identified her as a non-society player who sometimes wrote good-sized checks to charitable organizations. That put her and Doris, as retirees, on about the same level. Take your pick: the smart one or the affluent one.

Dene Hellman

Two things annoyed Sylvia about the children's museum. The children were darling, incredibly cute in fact, and well deserved the photos that their mothers and grandmothers were constantly taking. But there you had it—it cost several dollars to get a child in the door.

"What about the families that don't have the price of admission?" Sylvia sometimes said. Their kids would probably enjoy the museum even more than the favored clientele because they had never been to Disney World and never would have a chance to go. Most of their mothers were, generally, too busy trying to make rent money and grocery funds come out even with family need to give much thought to life enrichment, let alone birthday parties that included ponies to ride or trips to a children's museum.

The other thing that, to be vulgar about it, pissed Sylvia off was the way the whole bunch—young and old—treated the rabbit. The kids started poking at it right away and nobody stopped them. The Alice in Wonderland room was charming, what with all the costumes the kids could try on and the cut-out of Humpty Dumpty sitting on a wall but the rabbit was excess baggage. It obviously felt the same way and sat in one corner of its cage showing signs of life only with an occasional nose twitch.

Doris was in a hurry to leave, but Sylvia went in search of someone who looked as if she could make a decision. Having, the day before, looked up "rabbits as pets" on her computer, she said, "The bunny will have to be allowed out of its cage every day so it can get some exercise."

The in-charge person looked dubious. "I don't think that's possible," she said. "There is just too much mischief it can get into. We can't have it chewing on electric cords or leaving calling cards in the exhibits. We'll get somebody to feed it and clean the cage but that's as far as we can go."

When Sylvia moaned to Doris, over lunch, about her misgivings, Doris said she was making entirely too much of it. "I have the greatest confidence in the museum staff," she said. "They will have a meeting very soon and allocate some responsibilities."

Then Doris called the waitress over and told her that her sandwich had been made with the wrong bread. The waitress got all obsequious and, after apologizing profusely, brought Doris a sandwich that was much nicer. Then the manager came over to their table and asked Doris if everything was to her satisfaction.

Sylvia hated going out to eat with Doris because something like that always happened. Worse, even when it didn't, waiters and hostesses and managers singled Doris out as a Queen Bee while acting for all the world as if Sylvia was invisible. Maybe Sylvia's round face and short white hair were not stylish enough. She wondered about that, naturally, because Doris was thin and her well coifed blonde hair might signify some kind of superiority.

Actually, in this case, Sylvia's sandwich was not only on the wrong bread, it was entirely not the kind she had ordered and she hated herself, as well as Doris, because she failed to complain about it, thinking it might get the worried waitress in trouble.

"Why am I such a wuss?" she asked herself.

Now, however, Sylvia had some other thoughts that refused to be displaced by her awe of Doris. She didn't think the rabbit's welfare should be on hold until the museum people had a meeting. "You know what?" she said, "I'm going to make it a point to go over there every day or so and take the bunny outside so it can hop around."

Doris said she didn't think that was necessary and that she owed Sylvia an apology for getting her into a situation that caused her discomfort. Sylvia said that was all right and that, unlike Doris, she didn't have important things going on in her life so she had more time than Carter had pills. She added that she might even enjoy caring for the rabbit because her husband hadn't wanted them to have pets and now was a chance to make up for it.

Good as her word, the children's museum staff got used to seeing Sylvia slip in each day, gather up the rabbit and head out to the grassy area in back of the building. There she would sit, brandishing a carrot at the low energy animal that had acquired the name "Alice." Occasionally she could be seen scooping it up in her arms for a cuddle. After a half hour or so, during which Alice half-heartedly hopped around and nibbled at grass, Sylvia would gather her up and return her to the cage.

Some of the museum ladies said, "Awww," and some said, "What's going to happen when the weather turns cold?"

Doris came right out with it one evening when the two women were returning to their rooms after dinner. "Sylvia," she said, "do you want to spend that much time with the rabbit?"

Sylvia looked at her mutely and Doris knew right then that the rabbit might be a satisfactory pet for some but definitely not for everyone, Sylvia included. For whom, then? The next day she rode along when Sylvia went over to the museum and while Sylvia was out in the back stretch of grass with the rabbit, Doris asked for an impromptu meeting of all the volunteers present that day.

"We have a case of inhumane treatment on hand, and I don't mean the rabbit," she said. "What are we going to do about those two? Let's have some ideas; in fact, let's brain storm."

"Send Alice to the Humane Society."

"Make her into rabbit fricassee."

"Have a drawing, winner to get the rabbit."

"Donate her to the elementary school."

Clearly, Alice had failed to become popular because not a single person suggested taking turns exercising her, thus relieving Sylvia of her self-imposed task.

Doris thought there was merit to the idea of holding a contest to give away the rabbit and asked particulars of the woman who suggested it.

"Well," said Phyllis Oglivy, "when my son was in grade school, his class had a guinea pig. The teacher didn't know what to do with it over the summer so she announced that anyone who wanted to have "Oscar" during summer vacation should put his or her name in a box. The person whose name was drawn by the classroom assistant would get to take Oscar home on the last day of school. Unfortunately, my son "won" and came lugging the guinea pig home. We babysat that damn animal for two and a half months and when summer was over we tried to take it back to school but the teacher had gotten married and moved away. One of the kindergarten teachers finally accepted it, though, which was a relief."

"Sad story but good suggestion," said Doris.

An Alice contest was announced and a box for entries set up. Children were invited to paint pictures of Alice that would then be tacked up in the Animal Friends section of the museum. Books featuring rabbits were read aloud by a Theater Guild lady who happily read things aloud whenever anybody invited her to do so. This went on for two whole weeks, during which Sylvia continued devoting some of every day to Alice's needs.

When the entry box was opened, it contained only one name.

An extremely wealthy lady, Marcella Fontaine, who had brought her granddaughter to the museum the previous weekend, had put her name in the box. Everyone was in shock. "She has that gorgeous estate out on the edge of town," said Phyllis Oglivy. "She could buy a whole herd of rabbits if she wanted one. What does she want with Alice?"

Phyllis was charged with calling Mrs. Fontaine to inform her of her prize and couldn't resist sounding her out—under the guise of looking after Alice the Rabbit's welfare, naturally.

Mrs. Fontaine, who was so well connected that all of her friends lived in exciting places around the world, said that she didn't know any of the museum volunteers or Doris, the retired librarian, but that she was just thrilled. Her granddaughter Philippi often visited her and didn't have any animals in residence to enjoy at her grandmother's home because she had terrible allergies. Alice would solve that problem and would have her own little hutch in an enclosed pen behind the wisteria arbor where she could hop around all she wanted. The chauffer and the upstairs maid would look out for her when nobody else was in residence.

Phyllis reported this to the rest of the museum volunteers somewhat wistfully. Phyllis had five children between the ages of three and sixteen and, although the family was prosperous, she was tired. The thought of having her own little hutch and garden was delicious.

Doris broke the news of Alice-the-rabbit's future to Sylvia and asked her if she wanted to say goodbye. Sylvia thought to herself that she didn't find that necessary and was glad to have Alice's future taken care of. However, she gracefully thanked Doris for the suggestion and dutifully stroked Alice as the rabbit made her last hip-hop around the grassy plot behind the museum.

"I must learn to be a more compassionate person," said Doris to herself as she observed the parting.

"I must learn to be less of a patsy," said Sylvia to herself as she carried Alice inside for her last night at the museum.

Dene Hellman

PART THREE
A Strengthened Case

THE BASSO PROFUNDO COSSACK

WE SHIVERED WITH LISTENING PLEASURE on the Sundays when the choir director featured the voice of her prize male singer. After the service on those days, that performer smiled graciously or smugly—whichever interpretation you favor—as we made our ways out of the sanctuary. Being specially noticed was right up his alley so my failure to ever come up with a flattering remark was probably conspicuous.

His variety of deep dark bass, called "basso profundo," was cherished by Russian composers, by Mozart, by Handel, and by a lot of barbershop quartets.

At the time when my parents listened to group singing on television and on the radio, no cluster of singers was without its bottomless bass voice—the one that came on strong on the last line and made you laugh. (There probably were a couple of such singers entrenched in the champagne bubbles of Lawrence Welk. My mother could tell you.) Often, a man who was gifted with this voice was well into middle age with appropriately matured vocal cords. No wonder it isn't usual in today's song idols. They're either too young or too dead from their various indulgences.

I got to know the choir in the same way I knew other church members—superficially. If I was somewhat familiar with choir faces and manner, it's because I could sit in my pew, comfortable that courtesy actually called for staring at the singers during their performances. If the music was good, I was all ears. If it was only so-so, which happened from time to time, I analyzed the faces and body language of the singers. How individuals held their music folders told me quite a bit about them, as well as which ones badly needed an optometry appointment.

The bass and his wife came to most of the congregation's pot luck suppers and so did I. Those good humored collections of special dishes represented a significant part of the social life that I had, since the scoliosis of my adolescence resulted in an unsightly humped shoulder and my subsequent self-consciousness. As an adult, I live alone and am relatively unsocial except for my investment clients.

But I'd been raised as the only son in a family of women who were traditional homemakers and I get hungry for home cooking now that it's no longer part of my life. Therefore, on pot luck supper nights at the church I'd stop by KFC, pick up an immense order of fried chicken, and place it on the collective food table in the church's fellowship hall. It was eagerly eaten by the younger crowd, allowing me to dip deeply into the casseroles and pies without any sense of obligation.

My family—when I'd had a family—had been part of that church for generations. Some of the members knew that and often made it a point to make pleasant comments when they encountered me. Additionally, my substantial contributions to the treasury counted for something among those responsible for paying the congregation's bills. All in all, I felt relatively welcome but certainly not socially sought after.

The bass singer—okay, his name was Roger Webster—largely ignored me but his wife, Elizabeth, was a sweet lady who went out of her way to make me feel welcome even though she knew zilch about my history with the congregation or how much I gave to its general fund.

"You really like my scalloped potatoes," she'd say, smiling, and it wasn't hard to smile back at her and say she was the best cook, except for my Aunt Lucy, that I'd ever known.

On one such occasion, it came to my notice that Roger was a jealous type. Elizabeth smiled at me, and I smiled my compliments back and then realized that her husband, just across from us in the food line, had stiffened and was giving us a hard look. It must have quickly occurred to him that I, of all people, was nobody who would attract his wife or any other woman so he relaxed and even said, "How ya' doin'?" in my direction before sailing down the line scooping up double portions of dishes that appealed to him.

111

On one such night in late winter, he came over to the table where I was scarfing down a helping of green bean casserole and plunked himself in the vacant chair beside me. I looked at him inquiringly because he wasn't the kind of person who would do that just to be sociable.

He got right to the point.

"Whatcha doin' for fun these days?" he asked.

No business of his that I was in the midst of tax season and when it was over I was signed up for a *National Geographic* tour to the Galapagos that I looked forward to.

"Not much," was my reply.

"Got an offer you can't refuse," was his comeback.

I lifted an eyebrow in inquiry.

"You may not know," he said in a fake self-effacing voice, "that I'm involved in community theater."

Our local community theater isn't exactly Broadway or even off-Broadway. I'd stopped attending performances years before, tired of feeling personal embarrassment when somebody with no talent, diction or memory screwed up his lines. Besides, I was in New York often enough to know real theater.

So what did I say to Roger Webster, basso profundo of local note?

"You don't say!" uttered in a way that could be construed as awe or shock. Some kind of amazement, anyway.

Webster accepted my remark as benign.

"We got a problem," he said. "Our spring show is going to be a musical, like always, and this year it's a pretty ambitious project. We're doing *Heartbreak Village*."

Oh God, I thought. Not *Heartbreak Village*! A miserably pretentious musical that stirred *Fiddler on the Roof* up with *Les Miserable* and counted on audiences to love both of those enough to enjoy seeing yet one more 19th century village overrun by soldiers looting and murdering to music. I knew immediately which role Webster would sing: the demented head Cossack whose deep bass delivery made clear the extreme depths of his depravity.

"You don't say!" I remarked again, at a loss for a better comment.

Webster smirked.

"Yep! Quite a challenge there. Even my wife, Liz, is helping

112

out. She doesn't enjoy theater as much as I do, but she's agreed to be one of the villagers. Matter of fact, she thought you might do a little task for us."

Elizabeth had suggested me for something? An agreeable thought and one that encouraged me to go on listening.

At one time, about the time I was a sophomore in high school, I'd sung in the glee club because the music teacher said I had a nice voice. That activity fell away for good when I went on to the university and learned to conceal my self-consciousness about my deformity behind a computer. Should I try singing again, even in such a theatrical disaster as *Heartbreak Village*?

That little reverie ended abruptly when Webster explained why I would be useful. "The old theater is pretty much behind the times, ya know? We have to make do with some miserable sets and equipment. We just about shot the budget on this musical but it always gets real well attended in its two-weekend run so that makes up for it. And the rehearsals! Me and Liz rush home from work every night and grab a bite out of the fridge and then it's off to rehearsal. The guy who's been the curtain puller had to drop out— has to work late during this time of year. We'd appreciate your help filling in for him. How about it?"

He wanted me to stand in the wings to pull the stage curtains open and shut? Elizabeth had suggested me as a curtain puller?

My ego was always prepared for a little bruising, however, and my recovery time had grown briefer with each passing year.

"I'll think it over," I said, "and let you know on Sunday morning."

Webster grunted and got up from his chair. "Sure thing!" he said.

On my way out the door, I saw Elizabeth gathering up the empty dishes for their transfer to the kitchen dishwasher. She smiled at me. "Oh, Eugene," she said. "I'm going to keep my fingers crossed that you'll help us at the theater."

Sure thing.

The cast of *Heartbreak Village* had two weeks to go before opening night. They hadn't yet arrived at the point of dress rehearsals but were getting serious about using props, singing on key, and getting used to the various entrances and exits.

Dene Hellman

Elizabeth greeting me cordially when I put in my first appearance and never failed to acknowledge me on each succeeding night, but her interests seemed to be elsewhere. Her husband chose to totally ignore me. Neither made an effort to introduce me to other people who were there to sing and emote, to dance when it was called for. I told myself that I didn't mind; less acquaintance meant that instead of making polite noises I was free to indulge in the people watching that is one of the pleasures of my life. Sour grapes-like, I decided to treat the whole experience as a form of anthropology.

It amazed me that so many of Abbotsville's citizens wanted to be part of a community theater event. There was, it seemed, a good-sized representation of all the church choirs in town. Some of the local high school music teachers were also there and brought a few of their most promising students as well as kids who played in the school orchestra. There were, additionally, quite a few people who were inevitably going to come out for any local theatrics either because of devotion to the idea of local theater as a significant community asset—or because it gave them a platform for a social life of extraneous flirting and late evening partying. For sure, anybody who wanted a part in *Heartbreak Village* could have one because lots of "townsfolk" were needed for the chorus.

Since the musical had already been in rehearsal for some time, it was astounding that so many of the speaking roles were represented by people who, neglecting to learn their parts, carried their playbooks around and read from them when their lines came up. A kind of genial chaos was in effect.

Not so for the principal singers, of whom there perhaps four: the head Cossack sung by Roger Webster; the village Rabbi, sung by a man I didn't know whose beautiful tenor voice was a blessed addition to the cast, and a couple of tolerably voiced people in their late 20s (pretending to be teenagers) who made up the romantic interest. These four rehearsed and rehearsed, directed by Blane Roberts who was, in his daily life, the weatherman at KFOA. (Roberts, someone told me, had studied to be a music teacher but took up weather reporting because it paid better.)

Of this group of four, it was Roger Webster who penetrated every scene with suggestions that, inevitably, showcased him for more and better attention than anyone else would get.

114

"How would it be," he shamelessly asked Blane Roberts, "if instead of standing off to one side during the big village chorus I step up here on the gallows earlier as if they're all pleading and singing to me instead of to Jehovah?"

Roberts looked as if there were things he was tempted to say but then probably recalled what a pickle he'd be in if his basso profundo stomped off in a tizzy. He guessed the idea was okay, he said. Maybe he was used to performers who milked their roles for all the attention possible. Television stations likely had a lot of frustrated actors on their staffs.

Webster's big scene, just made bigger, was the one at the end of the second act where he stands on the gallows, having placed a breakaway noose around the neck of the village Rabbi, and bellows his offensive sentiments just before sending the poor victim to his gruesome fate. With his foot, he simultaneously activated the trap door opening to the pit into which the Rabbi fell. In the throes of his basso profundo-ness, theater goers would then surely give him a "BRAVO" and standing ovation in the best tradition of Russian Cossack musical history. He was probably correct in that assumption. Abbotsville is not a tough audience.

After the first week, I was confident of my function and timing as curtain opener and closer and, with one week to go before opening night, was well attuned to the dynamics of the Village Heartbreak participants. Consequently, I stopped watching the windbag antics of Roger Webster and focused on a few people who interested me—the Rabbi/tenor, for instance. His name, I learned, was Arnold Wister and he had lived in Abbotsville for only a few months. He had accepted a job managing the state arboretum that lay within a few miles of town and was hoping to meet some local people while he still had a bit of leisure.

One evening he walked over to introduce himself and I noticed that Elizabeth Webster headed my way, as well. She'd had ample time in the prior week to chat with me so I figured it was Arnold Wister, aka the Rabbi, who was the attraction.

I wasn't wrong in guessing the two of them were already acquainted. My little crush on Elizabeth, long suppressed, made me attentive to the attraction that blossomed in their mutual body language. I observed the light touches on the arm of the other that accompanied each comment. I listened to the mutual laughs that were meant to convey the casual nature of their conversation. I felt in my bones the appeal that each had for the other and wished them well although I thought Elizabeth's husband was inevitably going to weigh in on the situation.

At the ensuing dress rehearsal, with all the cast down to business at last, play books set aside, the would-be orchestra as complete as it ever was going to be, and Director Blane Roberts resigned to an "it is what it is" attitude, I stood in the wings beside the worn rope that controlled the curtain and looked across the stage to the opposite side. Most of the entrances and exits were going to be on my side of the stage and only Elizabeth and the Rabbi tenor stood on the opposite. My glance was at the wrong moment—at the exact second when Elizabeth put her arms around the neck of the Rabbi and he bent and kissed her. It was no flash of light flirtation or gesture of good wishes for the impending performance. It was a tender as a couple exchanging vows.

"Those two must have been at it for some time," I enviously mused.

If Roger Webster had seen anything of the kind, I knew, his response would have been uncontrollable rage. If he was always primed for the insult of someone taking his Liz away from him, what would he do if it was a fait accompli? Personally, I thought he had it coming if Elizabeth walked out on him but I'd seen enough of his ready jealousy to worry about the consequences. How was it possible, with his sharp sensitivities to his wife's every move, that he didn't know the threat posed by Arnold Wister, aka the Rabbi?

A total of four performances had been scheduled, two Friday evenings and two Saturday evenings. The first weekend went by without a hitch and Abbotsville ate up *Heartbreak Village* with unconditional enthusiasm. The singers, including Webster, were mostly on key and the large cast drew at least a half dozen relatives apiece so there was enough money coming in the door to assure the next theater season. I watched Elizabeth with concern that she and Wister keep their hearts away from their sleeves. They were inclined, it seemed to me, to think they were being cautious about their romance—but I could tell that quite a few of the cast had caught on and were also watching. Webster was, I hoped, so wrapped up in his own importance that he was, for once, oblivious to his wife's sentiments.

His big scene, the one in which he stood on the gallows singing to the villagers and the audience about his loathing for the Rabbi and all he stood for, really did bring down the house. People in the audience rose to their feet in acclamation when the deep bass tones tore through the auditorium and the Rabbi, strung up with his fake noose, dropped into the pit beneath the stage floor. All in questionable taste, I thought, considering the sentiments of the song, but nobody consulted me.

A word about the pit. It was a relic of the early years of the movie house, years when an organist seated at her instrument would rise up to stage level, playing her (it was nearly always a her) heart out in honor of whatever was happening on the screen. Quite a thrill at the time, I suppose.

The organ was long gone but the pit remained and once in a while it came in handy, as in allowing a white rabbit to pop in or out of a rabbit hole in a children's play or, as now, in hanging the Rabbi. It wasn't very deep and had been thoroughly padded to prevent injuries. Anyone spending time in it—before or after whatever rising or falling was called for—could descend via a few steps and exit through a door into a basement room that was currently being used for props.

The prop room was badly in need of reorganizing and sported a profusion of sofas, chairs and tables, not to mention numerous clothes racks holding the costumes of many seasons of plays. I averted my eyes when passing through, lest I be overcome with a compulsion to tidy things up.

Why did I have occasion to go there? The other thing about the basement area was that it had a men's room, albeit a seldom used one. Not one for superfluous socializing at a urinal, that was the toilet facility that I used when the evening was outlasting my bladder. I could slip away from my curtain manipulating duties when there was a pause, take a back stairway, use the men's room and be back upstairs in plenty of time.

I should have known that Webster would do nothing that would interfere with his theatrical importance, and was therefore lulled when three of the four performance nights went by with no evident awareness on his part concerning the affection between his wife and the tenor. On the fourth and last night, the Saturday evening that would end the presentation of *Heartbreak Village* and wrap up with a cast party that would send all the participants away to their more prosaic lives, I was still unconcerned. My one pervasive thought was that pulling tonight's stage curtain was the very last time I'd ever do so. The sociology of amateur theatrics would be forever out of my life and good riddance.

So, on the fourth evening, I watched offhandedly and listened indifferently as the villagers sang, the romantic duo sang, the Rabbi sang, the Cossacks sang. Then, when Webster and Wister stood on the gallows for their last great duet and Webster's basso profundo courtship of the audience, my attention was mainly focused on the speedy drawing of the curtain that would end the scene. If I'd been watching, would I have seen anything out of the ordinary?

Once the curtain was closed, I made a dash for the back stairway down to the basement men's room. I had, roughly, eight minutes before the third act curtain. How many of those eight were used to descend the stairway, cross the prop room, pee, wash my hands and emerge from the toilet? I took no chances and everything, including unzipping and zipping my pants, was performed with the utmost efficiency.

When I stepped from the men's room into the prop room on my return, I caught the merest glimpse of Roger Webster's back as he ascended the stairs to the back stage wing. He was moving fast and not likely to have seen me. Had he come down to the basement after I had, and why? My immediate assumption was that he'd come to retrieve a prop of some sort that he needed for the third act. A quick glance showed the room in its customary murkiness and the furniture and costumes in their standard disarray. It barely entered my consciousness that a couple of sofas were pushed up against the door that led to the organ pit but later, when I mentally reviewed those few seconds of observation, I saw them again and again in my mind's eye.

The third act curtain was duly opened and, when it closed at the end of the play, a huge outcry from the audience brought the cast out for curtain calls. My biceps, unused to much physical effort, felt the strain as I opened and closed the curtain again and again. A few of the cast, perhaps a few of the audience, noted the absence of Arnold Wister, who had sung the role of the Rabbi with such skill.

At the very end, when Webster was left alone on stage to bow and bow and bow to a crescendo of whistles and thunderous applause, Wister should have been with him but was nowhere to be seen. Determined to be on my way as soon as possible, I made a polite appearance at the cast party and then left after a short 15 minutes during which I nibbled a potato chip, refused a glass of second-rate wine, spoke pleasantly to anybody who happened to speak to me, and was out the door to the parking lot. Webster was in his element, hooting and laughing, downing a succession of drinks, poking other singers in the ribs. He totally ignored Elizabeth, who was standing off to one side looking worried. Her function would be to drive him home after the party.

"Have you seen Arnold?" she asked me, just before I walked out.

I shook my head. "Probably doesn't care much for parties," was my answer.

"Probably was insulted to the point of furious indignation by your husband," was what I silently said to myself.

Sunday passed. On Monday, someone's review of *Heartbreak Village* was published in the *Abbotsville Times* under the title *Village Delight*. The "wonderful music" that the town had been privileged to experience was lovingly and specifically noted: Roger Webster and Arnold Wister were singled out for extra accolades. The reviewer didn't extol one more than the other, which was astute on his/her part, but readers were given to understand that no community anywhere in the country could experience better voices. Additionally, the set design was complimented and there was even an exposition about the theater's history and the uses to which the organ pit had been put at various times over the years.

On Tuesday, the public was informed that Arnold Wister, who had sung the role of the Rabbi in *Heartbreak Village*, was missing. He hadn't shown up at the arboretum on Monday and there were no signs he had been in his apartment for a couple of days. Anyone with information as to his whereabouts should notify the local police.

On Wednesday, the *Abbotsville Times* had a scoop. Big headlines told the reading public that when the prop committee of *Heartbreak Village* had gone over to the theater on Tuesday evening to break down the stage set for storage, they had discovered Wister's body in the organ pit.

The state newspapers took up the story, as did television, complete with somebody's amateur video—probably taken at the last dress rehearsal—of Wister and Webster singing their big duet just before Wister tumbled into the pit with a fake noose around his neck. Webster must have been thrilled. With publicity like that, who could wish for more? He would have, I thought, been happy to exchange Wister's life for some good shots of himself, Webster, belting out an aria that was now disseminated to the entire country.

Later, it was announced that Wister had died of a broken neck but it wasn't due to the phony breakaway noose. He'd probably fallen wrong and the rope had twisted in some odd way; it was a bizarre accident and death had surely been immediate.

All in all, I was relieved to get my clients and myself through the remaining tax season and then check in for the Smithsonian tour. Such excursions are what keep me going in life. As long as they last, they leave me with little time for self-pity over my misshapen body. The other tour participants are, like me, interested in what makes the world go round, not in the personal deficiencies of their short-term companions. Sometimes, as with this tour, there is a lonely lady who is not averse to sharing a bit of a dalliance.

Still, at odd moments I would think about Wister's strange accident and replay my glimpse of the back of Webster's frame, clad in his Cossack uniform, cap, gloves and boots included, moving rapidly up the stairway to the main floor of the theater.

I began asking myself questions.

*How did Webster get down the back stairs of the basement? My last glimpse of him had been when I closed the second act curtain. He'd been standing on the gallows and would step down only when the stage was fully obscured. I had turned my back on it all as I quickly headed for the stairway to the basement and the men's lavatory but, even though I moved at a good clip, he had managed to get downstairs, do whatever he wanted to do, and be on his way up when I came out of the washroom.

*If he had killed Wister, how could it be executed so speedily?

*Who moved the sofas against the door that led to the organ pit? Was it Webster? Why would he do that?

Damn it, Webster had for sure killed Arnold Wister. I knew why; he had caught on to the attraction between Elizabeth and Wister and was jealous. The real question was how he managed to do the job. It had been declared an accident by the investigators but, when I went over and over the details in my mind, I always got stuck. How did he get off that gallows and down the stairs so fast? Presumably, it takes a moment or two to kill somebody so speed was of the essence. Yet, if he'd been right behind me on the stairway, I would have heard him.

Eventually, it occurred to me: Webster hadn't taken the stairs down. He'd jumped off the gallows directly into the pit where Wister had fallen. But wouldn't someone have seen him do that? Probably. There were other cast members on the stage milling around as they made their exits through one wing or another. Most of them wouldn't have been paying any attention to Webster but at least one or two, his wife for sure, would have seen him jumping into the organ pit. It wouldn't have been a remarkable thing to do, since the pit made for a quick exit to the prop room—but what about later in the week when Wister's death was known?

Anybody who was thinking the evening over and arriving at *what if* questions would, also like me, keep it to themselves as a Pandora's box that should remain firmly closed. Besides, I liked Elizabeth Webster well enough to want to avoid dragging her name and possible attachment to Wister into public view.

My personal scenario was that, pressed for time, Webster actually fixed the noose so he could hang Wister on stage, while singing loudly and deeply. Then, at the conclusion of the second act, he'd jumped into the organ pit and unfastened the noose. Not much time required for that, even for somebody wearing Cossack gloves, as he was. Another few seconds and he could get out through the door into the prop room, push a couple of sofas up against the door to discourage snooping, and be on his way up the stairs in plenty of time for the third act curtain.

This conjecture wasn't provable and it made no sense for me to share it with anyone.

Back from my Galapagos tour by the end of May, I appreciated the fact that Arnold Wister's story was out of the local news. It would haunt me forever, I knew, but if the authorities chose to regard it as an odd happenstance, what could I say? All I had was a conjecture.

I changed churches, sincerely hoping to never again lay eyes on Roger Webster, his wife, the entire choir, or one of the congregation's pot luck events. (The new church turned out to be a good choice, with its strong inclination toward friendly socializing. I can't say there are many first-rate cooks among its members but affability and good will make up for it.)

Six months passed and then the local newspaper published a dreadful story. Elizabeth Webster had fallen down her basement stairs on Saturday evening and was dead. Her sister, Kathryn, had discovered her when she'd come over the next day to watch *Downton Abbey* with her, as was their Sunday evening custom. The investigators decreed an accident because the light bulb on the stairway was burned out and the second step from the top was loose. Elizabeth had been carrying an armload of laundry meant for the basement washer and perhaps had tripped on a dangling shirt-tail just as the stair step had given way. Her husband had not been home at the time of death—or so he said—and, in truth, several of his friends could attest to his presence that evening in the local pub. He also claimed to have gone directly to bed when he came home and stayed in bed most of Sunday, sleeping off his intake of booze. He had never thought to look for his wife.

Two days later, there was a bold front-page story in a lot of newspapers.

Elizabeth's sister, it said, had reported that Elizabeth was scared to death of her husband. He was becoming more and more restrictive about her free time, accusing her of all sorts of romances with her co-workers and even threatening to kill her if she left him. Kathryn said that her sister had called her, sobbing, on Saturday morning, the day she died. Roger had hinted that he'd killed Arnold Wister the previous spring and it was her fault for being such a whore. Elizabeth swore Kathryn to secrecy, saying that she almost believed the part about killing Arnold but maybe it was just said to frighten her.

Webster was picked up, charged in the murder of his wife and the investigation that should have taken place when Arnold Wister's body was discovered in the organ pit was hastily conducted. Additionally, the basement step in the Webster house showed it had been tampered with and would have easily yielded if someone had given Elizabeth a small shove from behind. Some of Webster's pals belatedly recalled that Roger had seemed upset when he arrived at the pub and had become especially boisterous and incoherent in his conversation.

There was a trial and a few surprising witnesses from the cast of Village Heartbreak came forward. Like me, they'd had some afterthoughts about Wister's accident because they recalled seeing him jump into the organ pit at the end of the second act. It was all hearsay so all that was accomplished was a strengthened case against Roger Webster with regard to his wife's death.

But the video of him and Arnold Wister belting out their song on the gallows during dress rehearsal was too good for the media to pass up and it had a good many national airings. No doubt, I thought, Webster was sufficiently gratified about the publicity to overlook the inconvenience of being convicted of second degree murder.

He got a good, stiff sentence and was hauled off to prison. Thoughts ranging from my acceptance of curtain-pulling duty to Elizabeth's death and on to Webster's trial and sentence weighed on me greatly, but I was gratified that there would now be closure.

The closure lasted about a year.

Then there was a cute little anecdote in one of the larger state newspapers that Webster had gotten permission from the warden of his particular prison to form a prison chorus.

The warden was an enlightened individual and had already approved a group that was interested in learning professional horticulture and another that was developing expertise in training dogs to assist medically disadvantaged veterans. Why not a chorus?

Sunday supplements did a feature story.

There were, it seemed, a good many prisoners who liked to sing and were enthusiastic about doing more of it. Webster's chorus became a reality and a music professor from a nearby university volunteered his time to conduct. Webster's voice was a happy contribution to the group because who doesn't get a kick out of a basso profundo? Plus, his prior publicity gave them an advantage.

Another year went by. The chorus was featured now and again at some event, with the participants as well-guarded as any crew out picking up trash from roadways even though its members were judged to be very low risk.

In no time, I speculated, women would be offering to marry the single singers and showing up for conjugal visits.

In yesterday's Times, I saw that a (now renowned) chorus from an east coast penitentiary, showcasing singers that include convicted murderer Roger Webster and his gorgeous deep bass, would be featured on one of national television's Sunday evening news magazines.

I like good music as much or more than the average person but the whole scenario makes me sick to my stomach. This year, I have decided that I will forego my usual season tickets to the operas that tour our state's larger auditoriums Those Russian composers were altogether too fond of their basso profundos for my peace of mind.

STUD MUFFIN

WAYNE NEVER WAS HIMSELF after they closed the lid on Vera's coffin. Even though he was given to angry outbursts, he watched with what his neighbors and family thought was an impassive expression. This apparent impassiveness was retained throughout the ceremony at the cemetery and the reception that took place afterward.

"I kept waiting for him to confront the undertaker and insist that Vera should be put in a different grave," said one person who had known him for several decades.

Vera had been Wayne's wife for over 50 years so it should be no surprise that he had come to rely on her for much of what he thought and did. Still, nobody had been aware of how much that dependence was the case because Wayne had a mouth on him and used it wherever he went. If any of his acquaintances suspected that he was a ventriloquist's dummy manipulated by Vera, they never let on.

Through the years, whenever a neighbor or someone at the church or a town official saw Wayne coming, they knew they were in for a complaint that carried ugly overtones. Vera, on the other hand, posed as a pious lady who instigated numerous prayer circles dedicated to the morals and traumas of the town's citizens. In general, her salacious interest was no better appreciated than Wayne's outspoken venom.

Between them, they addressed a great deal of local life. If a woman was suspected of improper behavior with somebody else's husband, here came a prayer circle, begun by Vera, seeking to amend the suspicious behavior. If the sewer backed up on the east side of town, here came Wayne to demand retribution and correction from the town council. If a neighbor's barbecue smoke blew toward Wayne's and Vera's back yard, the neighbor knew his picnic would be interrupted by a tirade launched from just outside his property line by a ferocious Wayne.

But, no matter how much the couple's disagreeable interference crossed the line of normally accepted courtesy, people didn't complain as much as they wanted to. "Better to agree with 'em than argue," they said. Over the years, it got so whatever folks thought of doing, they'd mentally review it with a hypothesis of what Wayne and Vera would think of it.

Trees were planted or cut down, streets were paved or not, school buses stopped at one corner or in the middle of the next street—all decisions made in deference to the potential opinions of the terrible two.

The very month before Vera fell backward off her treadmill and tumbled down to a finale of broken bones and brain concussion, she complained to Wayne that the next door neighbors were having a lot of company and the various cars driven by those guests were being parked next to the curb that ran past Wayne and Vera's house.

"That space ought to be for our company," she said.

Of course, they never had any company. Their two daughters came to visit once in a while, when it couldn't be delayed any longer, but the girls parked in the driveway. Usually, they came together in one car because their husbands and now-grown kids refused to participate in the dutiful ritual.

"You kidding me?" said the husbands when they were urged to accompany their wives. "All I'd hear is that I don't make enough money and that we need to paint the house."

Despite infrequent competition for parking spaces, after the next perceived invasion of their curb space, Wayne raged down the street to present his protest and yelled at the neighbor's guests when they arrived. "Find another place to park! You got no right to hog the whole street!"

This happened more than once.

In the background, Vera nodded her head in satisfaction. "You tell 'em!" she said. "If they want to entertain every Tom, Dick and Martha they know, they gotta know that the rest of us have rights."

After Vera's bad accident, people were more overt in their discussions. Cathy Withers had gone to school with both Vera and Wayne and offered a new perspective on the couple. "Wayne was always considered a pretty nice guy," she said. "He never had a whole lot to say, but was generally liked. Vera, on the other hand, was a real snip. She carried grudges that she made up out of thin air. If there was a rumor against somebody, it likely could be traced back to her. When she and Wayne started going together, we were kind of surprised."

Most of the townspeople at least feigned sympathy when Vera died from her fall, more for the sake of her daughters than anything. The girls were grateful and even wondered a little bit if their parents had more friends than they'd let on. The big concern was what to do with their father. He had always taken care of the outdoor chores and any needed repairs around the house but left the running of the household entirely to Vera. Their income was limited to two Social Security checks, but that was enough to take care of their simple needs. Now, however, there was a problem. Vera's check would be a thing of the past and Wayne couldn't cook and had never balanced a budget. The house was his, free and clear, but there would still be taxes and heating bills, not to mention upkeep on a barely adequate car. A resolute conservative, he had spent years decrying food stamps and Medicaid; he most certain would never apply for either, regardless of need.

"He'll have to sell the house and take turns living with us," the daughters said. Their husbands begged to differ.

"You trying to drive me out?" each said to his spouse. "He'd find fault with everything I do, every beer I drink, every conversation I have over the backyard fence." Each wife acknowledged the truth of this and agreed, at last, that Dad would have to go into the Fine Neighbors nursing home.

As nursing homes go, Fine Neighbors was a pleasant one. It had been needed for a long time, as the townspeople aged in place and a lot of local families just didn't have the wherewithal to keep their parents at home. Those days were over, they had to agree. Everybody had a job now, but the jobs didn't pay enough to hire in-home nurses. When a parent got forgetful and let the eggs boil dry on the stove, a house could go up in flames so that was always a worry. The very cost of keeping houses at the hot-house temperatures required by aging bodies was astronomical.

When some of the important businesspeople of the town got a grant and lined up government support, the nursing home was built and it was a very nice place that deserved its name. There was medical care when it was needed, there were decent meals, there was an activity bus that weekly ran nursing home occupants around to their doctors. There was even a recreation director who came in for three days a week to encourage card playing and group singing.

Almost all the residents knew one another and either retained their ongoing relationships or, sometimes, found friends among people they had heretofore ignored. More than one romance caught fire and semi-scandalized the community. There weren't enough men to go around, of course, but many of the women residents accepted that with grace. "Been there; done that," they'd say. "What do I want with some old coot who probably wears diapers?"

Wayne saw no good in the nursing home setup but he didn't like his sons-in-law any better than they liked him. Besides, he was tired of eating tinned sardines and pre-packaged cinnamon rolls and trying to keep ants out of the pantry during rainy spells. He didn't have much to say when the Fine Neighbors arrangements were made, other than complaining when told that his Social Security check would have to go toward his upkeep and, additionally, have to be supplemented by various other government programs. His house would have to be sold and whatever modest price that brought would also have to be thrown into the kitty.

"Paid taxes all my life and now they're takin' my house! Ain't it about time the guv-ment gave somethin' back?" he snarled.

He continued to complain, long after his daughters settled him into the nursing home. Forced into sharing a room with Macy Hilbert, with whom he had never had an easy relationship, he made up his mind that he had zilch to say to anybody and nobody had anything of value to say to him. He accepted the blood pressure medicine that the nurse handed out without giving her so much as an acknowledging grunt. He refused to go to the communal dining room for what he considered disgusting meals and those often sat on the tray table beside his bed until someone took them away. Before long, he took to a wheel chair but could maneuver himself into the bathroom when he needed to relieve himself and usually managed to get to the big television set in the lounge before anybody else so he could be certain that Fox News was the channel of choice.

Except for bed and bath times, activities he also performed without help, Wayne sat in passive irritation in his wheel chair for nearly two years. When the daughters visited, which they always did as a pair, he "let them have it good" as Vera would have said, about the unacceptability of his life. They usually left the nursing home in tears, a circumstance that Wayne appeared to find quite satisfactory.

His behavior did not go unnoticed by the Fine Neighbors Board of Directors, most of whom had known him for years and who now said, "What can be done? He's always been like that and he just has to go on doing what he's always done and the staff will have to put up with it!"

One of the Directors was a lady who had arrived in town during recent years, bringing with her such an aura of prosperity and wisdom that she shortly became one of those described by the locals as "running things." It was approximately the truth and that lady now said, "But what a shame! There must be some way to give him a more positive outlook!"

She received no response and the meeting soon adjourned although she remained thoughtful and later consulted one or two former colleagues who lived and worked in senior services in another town.

It was never known who sent Wayne the balloons. It wasn't his birthday and it wasn't a holiday and the delivery person was from the bigger town up the road and didn't know Wayne at all. It might have been a joke but, if so, it was an expensive joke and hardly anybody had that kind of money to throw away on an old guy in a wheel chair who didn't have a friend in the world. One thing for certain, it was not a wrong delivery. Each of the balloons was printed with a personal message. "Love to a Stud Muffin," said one. "Wayne—one hot dude," said another. The other balloons were equally rakish in their sentiments.

The daytime receptionist tied the bouquet to the arm of Wayne's wheel chair.

"You have a secret admirer!" she exclaimed, and the rest of the Fine Neighbor's staff followed suit, teasing and coaxing. "You must have an idea who sent 'em," they said. "Give us a hint!"

All of this was met with the most meager of grunts on Wayne's part. He knew the daughters wouldn't have sent the balloons. Hell, they hardly put in an appearance on his birthday, and never brought their husbands with them. The grandkids didn't seem to even know who he was, which was okay with him since he thought they all had miserable manners and barely enough brains to keep themselves out of the county jail.

Still, when one of the more attractive of the grey-haired women who watched television in the evenings said, very shyly, "Wayne, do you have a girl friend?" he allowed himself a tiny, sly little smile.

The woman, who really had a pair of pretty dimples on her face, later told everybody in the dining room, "Wayne as much as admitted to me that he has a lady friend. I don't know who she is, but maybe he visits her when we think he's at the medical clinic!"

Before he knew what was happening, the other resident ladies started flirting with him in the television lounge. Then a couple of them cajoled him into going with them to the dining room, which turned out to be a more satisfactory place to eat than the edge of his bed had been. When the recreation director got the residents playing catch with one another, to better their coordination, Wayne had so many balls tossed in his direction that he had to use all his might to return each to its donor lady. He began saying thank you to the nurse when she brought his blood pressure pill because she really was fairly nice looking as well as being a kindly individual. In no time at all, he was playing Bingo and dealing cards. He started telling jokes and teasing people, even the sullen kid who did odd jobs.

"A regular stud muffin!" the nurse reported to the Fine Neighbors manager. "Next thing you know, we'll be pulling him out of somebody's bed!"

The manager reported this turn of events at a Fine Neighbors Board of Directors' meeting. The directors let this pass with a mild shake of their heads and comments to the effect that it was good to have at least one problem solved.

The woman who had said at a prior meeting that surely something could be done to give Wayne a more positive outlook on life, didn't say anything but looked down at her meeting agenda with a mysterious smile of satisfaction.

The daughters didn't like Wayne's new behavior one bit. "What's gotten into him?" they asked one another. "What would Mother have thought of this new development?" was another question and they decided that their father, depressed over Vera's passing,, was sinking into a know-nothing dementia.

Cathy Winters, the woman who had gone to high school with Vera and Wayne, begged to differ. "Wayne was sort of jovial until Vera got her hooks into him and showed him how to behave. One doesn't like to speak ill of the dead, but maybe Wayne is ,just getting back to his normal self now that Vera's gone."

Eventually, Wayne's grandkids forgot what kind of person they had thought he was during the years when they were growing up and once in a while they brought one of their babies over to Fine Neighbors and said, "Look at your great grandson! He looks just like your baby picture!"

The grey-haired lady with the pretty dimples said she certainly could see it, the new baby was the very image of Wayne. The rest of the ladies agreed and even the nurse said it was true. "Going to grow up and wow the womenfolk!" she said.

Wayne smiled a contented smile although he couldn't recall wowing many of the women he'd known over the course of his lifetime. "Maybe Vera always chased 'em off," he mused. It was getting harder to envision Vera in his mind's eye but once in a while, when he was having a good time, he had an uneasy feeling that, like her daughters, she might not approve of his Fine Neighbors lifestyle.

"Nothing to be jealous about," he said to her shadow image when it rose up in his mind "If a guy enjoys a little attention from the ladies every now and then, it just helps the world go around. Sometimes a person just has to go along to get along!"

Dene Hellman

OH, THOSE GOSSAMER WINGS

WILLIAM WESLEY CANFIELD WROTE BOOKS of lyrical intensity. That's what an early critic said and the appellation stuck. Canfield's books tended to be about people similar to himself who lived in peculiar circumstances. These circumstances, in turn, were hosts to a wide variety of adjectives and metaphors so subterranean that a lot of paragraphs had to be read several times to extract their meaning.

The first book was about an adrift journalist who photographed in dangerous places, was subsequently taken captive, and was forced by his jailers to live in solitary confinement for several years—valid subject matter, for sure. The confinement spot was a deep cave with sensory attributes that eventually drove the journalist mad.

So deeply thrust, so waxed the wings of emanate birds
that moved harkingly into a crystal pavilion of thought
that immersed his visions of home into a cocoon of
silken thread, unceasingly knitting up and forever
unraveling into fine spikes of silver dust.

Thus wrote William Wesley Canfield and, not far behind him, the New York Times book reviewer wrote in a piece that sounded as if the critic was determined to, by God, show off his own crystal pavilion of thought. Either that or he had no good idea of what the book was about and made his review as hazy as possible so nobody could catch him unawares.

A lot of people bought the book, some of them read it, and most gave up on it about a third of the way into the pages. A well-known actor optioned the book, which was nicely titled *Nine Stitches Saved*. There were Pulitzer Prize murmurs. Intellectuals hailed it as evidence of a great new talent that would someday keep Faulkner company in textbook discussions.

Subsequently, William, the author, and his wife, Carolyn, bought a very nice house in the oldest, most genteel part of town.

He quit his day job as editor at the community magazine headquarters but Carolyn continued in her career as math and chemistry teacher so they could pay their bills if there were no more books. They already had a baby, a little girl named Ariel, whom William loved but never did get to know. (She grew up being told she should not interrupt him at his work in his studio; William dutifully attended her high school and college graduations and walked her down the aisle when she got married but found her exceedingly puzzling.) Year after year, William ran several miles in early morning hours, came home to eat breakfast with Carolyn, and saw her off to her teaching job before showering and retreating to his studio. Life was good. The occasional magazine article, semester of teaching at a college, or lucrative summons to read at a big city library supplemented their income nicely.

The second book, which came along four years later, was about a man who saw his fiancé only one night each week, all the while pursuing his compulsion to paint, and who became so involved in his work that he didn't notice when the lady disappeared, possibly into one of his canvases. This book, *Gathered Moss Rolling*, actually was made into a film. As the murmurs continued with respect to a Pulitzer, some thought the widely publicized film compared positively with Ingmar Bergman's *The Seventh Seal*. It won accolades at several film festivals and was shown in some of the more distinguished art houses, but rarely grossed enough to cover its expenses. The book was reputed to sell quite well although one of the accountants at William's publishing house said he suspected cartons of it were being shipped to far-away places in Asia and left moldering on docks until thrown into the recesses of warehouses. Still, "seven months on bestseller lists" had a nice ring to it.

The third book—*Later Than Never*—was about a successful businessman who vanished from sight, at his own choice, and who then had esoteric experiences in out-of-the-way South American and European art galleries.

Writing with lyrical intensity is damn hard work, so that one was published several years after the second.

During the between years, when not earning money doing the things that successful writers earn money doing, William sat in his study reading books written by other people, sketching funny characters on the backs of discarded manuscript pages, and paging through dictionaries in search of interesting words. Sometimes, metaphors occurred to him and he stockpiled them for use in future books. His marriage to Carolyn continued along quite well. They ate together, shared a bedroom and discussed current events. Neither of them had affairs, drank too much, or voted for opposing candidates.

Later Than Never wasn't an unqualified success. The reviewers introduced a few caveats into their comments. University English teachers, who until now were among the few to read a Canfield book from start to finish began to grumble to each other.

"I tell you," said Dr. E. Ubis Martin of Smith to his counterpart at Brown, "the damn thing is so dark that I wanted to kill myself by the end of the fourth chapter. And the worst of it was, I didn't even understand why I was so miserable."

"I know what you mean," was the rejoinder. "Made me wonder why I was putting up with that kind of abuse. It was sort of like getting shut in the basement by my stepfather all over again."

When *Later Than Never* came off the bestselling book list in less than four weeks, even William got the message. After two weeks of alternately scribbling words and line drawings, he said to Carolyn, "I'm tempted to try my hand at a graphic novel!"

With characteristic cheeriness, Carolyn said, "Go for it! My teacher's pension will kick in two or three years from now and we can always sell the house."

In Carolyn's view, the dubious reception of *Later Than Never* was overshadowed by a perfectly wonderful event—the birth of their grandson. Not a daddy's girl, for obvious reasons, Ariel named her son "Dwight" rather than "William." William accepted that in stride, not giving the matter any thought even though Carolyn was miffed. It was hard, however, for him to take to Dwight with conventional pride. At first, the small being was a nonentity. Later, when Dwight was old enough to sit in a high chair to be fed disgusting purees, William watched with horror as the child ate/spit/absorbed spinach and other messy vegetable concoctions. On the occasion of one of Ariel's and Dwight's visits to her parents, this went on at the dinner table, causing William to push back his chair and ascend to his writing studio.

According to Carolyn and Ariel, Dwight was "advanced." He walked at ten months and began saying words when he was less than a year old. By 18 months, he could count to five and by age two he knew his colors. He had also learned that one did not go upstairs and bother "Grand," his word for William (which seemed to amuse Carolyn and Ariel no end and, annoyingly, they, as well, took to addressing him as "Grand").

One afternoon, however, when Ariel and Carolyn were absorbed in admiring a volunteer clematis vine in the front garden, Dwight looked at the interesting staircase that rose from the entry hall.

"Up," he said, and began a labored climb.

At the top, he followed light until he came to William's study.

"Book," he stated, as he stood in the doorway staring at his startled grandfather.

"Good choice of words," said William Wesley Canfield, author of three books that had almost won Pulitzers.

"Book," repeated Dwight Canfield Osgood. He said it with great firmness.

Rising to his feet, William walked over to his enormous library of books and beckoned Dwight to stand beside him. Together they looked upward, staring at the hundreds and hundreds of volumes.

"Did you have a particular one in mind?" William asked. He took a copy of his first, *Nine Stitches Saved*, from a prominent spot. "I can recommend this one if you have a little time."

"NO!" said Dwight. "BOOK!"

Not being entirely without grandfatherly instinct, William perceived that Dwight wished to be shown a colorful child's book. He had once seen Ariel reading to her son and had thought it made a charming picture. In fact, in Ariel's early childhood days, she had owned and been read to (by Carolyn) a good many books that ranged from renderings of trains and kittens to the later machinations of precocious spiders.

Those books might be somewhere in the house. Carolyn wasn't a pack rat but he'd seen with amusement how she held on to certain artifacts of their earlier years. "Let's go find one," he said to Dwight, offering his hand.

None of the empty bedrooms, even Ariel's old room, housed any children's books. Steering Dwight into the bedroom he and

Carolyn shared, William observed with astonishment that Ariel's childhood library was taking up space on the shelves of an antique bookcase that always stood just where it now was. He hadn't given it a glance in—*how many years?*

Dwight threw himself at the books, holding out his arms as if to embrace them all. "Book!" he said.

"If you feel that way, said William, "you should learn to use the plural form. Books with an 's'!"

By this time, Dwight had extracted three of the books and maneuvered his posterior toward William, who had sat down on an easy chair in order to put the shelves closer to eye level. William welcomed his grandson onto his lap and recognized it was a cue to begin reading aloud. The material wasn't without its charms, including accounts of a woman who lived in a shoe, trains that went every which way, mostly up, and one that consisted of tirelessly bidding a good night to all kinds of animate and inanimate objects.

Carolyn and Ariel found them there somewhat later, both fast asleep. Ariel gently carried Dwight to her car, strapped him into his car seat, and drove home. When William awoke, he found Carolyn sitting on the bed, smiling at him.

"Got through to you, did he?" she asked.

Finding no logical response to this, William followed his usual inclination, which was to discuss books. "Carolyn," he said, "I had no idea! These things are quite delightful. Although I find some of them a bit short of talent. Book and drawing by two different people! I mean, with elementary text like that it must take a lot of nerve to expect somebody else to illustrate the story."

"Think you could do better?" asked Carolyn, who after all these years knew when to challenge her husband and when to keep her mouth shut.

Two weeks later, when Ariel brought Dwight over for a sunny afternoon's visit with her parents, William was ready for them. Ready for Dwight, to be exact. He had folded sheets of paper together to form a book, a book that included story and pictures by William Wesley Canfield.

"Book!" he said triumphantly, displaying it at Dwight's eye level.

Looking a bit skeptical, Dwight plopped himself down beside

William on a patio settee and waited for a literary experience to begin.

William read, with great expression, a story about a firefly. The illustrations, while eccentric, were amazingly appealing. The text said the firefly's wings were gossamer. This infuriated Dwight.

"ORANGE!" he said.

"GOSSAMER!" said William.

"ORANGE!" shouted Dwight, looking as if he would climb down from the settee any minute if Grand persisted in this ridiculous idea.

"Okay, *orange*," said William. He blotted out the word "gossamer" on the spot and superimposed "orange" over it. This procedure went on to the very end of the story. Dwight objected to "verdant," "azure," and "luminous," and settled for "green," "blue," and "shiny." William felt rather as he had in English 101 when his professor cracked down on him for writing that someone spoke in stentorian tones. "Trite!" the teacher said, not realizing that William would go on to write books of lyrical intensity that would almost be awarded Pulitzers.

"I like doing the pictures," William said to Carolyn that evening when she asked him where he was going with this strange little twist and was he just killing time until he came up with a new book idea?

"Plots that feature art always seem to figure big in my books," he said. "When I'm not writing, I always find myself drawing little pictures. Did that 'way back in Junior High. It's time I explore that tendency."

The next week, he went to the local art store and bought some quality watercolors plus a full array of colored pencils. It took about a month of experimentation to decide which he would use in his illustrations. That settled, he began a story about a ladybug and a Dalmatian who were in competition. He had a wonderful time painting spots of one kind or another and when he finished and showed it to Carolyn, she said, "You know what? There's joy sticking out all over these pages. I do believe you have captured something lyrical for real!"

Thus encouraged, William debated with himself whether or not to show it to his publisher. Deciding in the affirmative, he was going to put his name on the cover page and then thought that, under the circumstances, "William Wesley Canfield" looked to be in the same category as "stentorian" and "gossamer." Across the front cover, he printed "WILL CANFIELD" just under the title YOUR SPOTS, MY DOTS.

The publisher loved the book and the whole idea of such a notable writer of serious books coming up with such an astonishing contribution to children's literature. He also recognized the market value of such a switch and assigned his publicists the task of making it known to the literary world. The reviews were unqualified, hailing YOUR SPOTS, MY DOTS as a plea for cultural tolerance that somewhat brought to mind the chorus of Handel's *Messiah*.

Bypassing talk of a Pulitzer, a Nobel began to be suggested. Never had one of William's books gone through so many printings or been purchased by so many libraries, schools and grandmothers. Folks who were in the know would say to one another, "It's hard to believe but this Will Canfield is the same guy who wrote all those so-called literary masterpieces under the name "William Wesley Canfield."

The English professor at Brown said to T. Zarathustra Martin, his associate at Smith, "What got into the guy?" and the professor at Smith said, cynically, "Bad reviews, maybe?"

At home, William persisted on a high state of elation that Carolyn hoped he'd maintain. The entire country seemed to be awaiting another book for children and that meant he didn't hang out in his studio except when he wanted to paint or put together another story. He was out exploring the world of birds, bees and vegetation, looking for inspiration.

He had enough sense to know that the complexity of his books would have to rise each year according to what level of reading Dwight had reached—until such time as Dwight was lost to the world of soccer. Characters would have to be better defined and the plots more complex. In time, he would need to write something closer to *Wind in the Willows* than YOUR SPOTS, MY DOTS.

He stood in front of his library of books one evening in much the same pose that he and Dwight had stood months before. It now included shelves of children's classics, from *Black Beauty* to *Charlotte's Web*.

You know what?" he said to the essence of E.B. White that floated before his eyes. "I have some writing years left—and just you wait! My lady bug is, for sure, going to outshine your spider!"

JUNK MAIL

BOOM BOOM BOOM. TA RAH DA. The whole town watched on crisp autumn mornings when the Millwell High School marching band swung down the street, Roberta Lotzberger prancing ahead of it, throwing her baton up in the air with great skill and catching it with a triumphant smile that warmed the hearts of all who watched. Millwell's new band instructor, Mr. Hoffman, thought marching on real streets gave his band members good experience with the chemistry of having onlookers.

Doc Pinster, the local dentist, took more of an interest in the local band than did Manny Streeter, postmaster. Manny listened to opera on Saturday afternoons so sometimes the muscles in his jaw got a little tense during Millwell High's marching band practices on Main Street. Doc, on the other hand, had no great feel for music but took pride in the smiles that Roberta Lotzberger flashed at the local onlookers. Doc tended to judge everybody by his or her teeth.

"A real beauty," said Doc, giving credit to other aspects of Roberta's appearance but particularly concentrating on her smile. Concerned in her early adolescence about her tendency to protruding teeth, Doc had encouraged her parents to take her over to Fort Dodge for orthodontic work. Thus, he felt a certain responsibility for her good looks.

Manny was not inclined to give much thought to young women, including Roberta, but had seen her come into the post office often enough over the years to give credit where it was due. He had heard talk from many a local person that Roberta was pretty enough and talented enough to get into the movies. It was said that she had done a wonderful job playing the lead in the Junior class play the autumn before and would surely be just as good playing the lead in the Senior play next spring.

She could have been competition for Sarah Bernhardt for all Manny knew because he never went over to the high school gymnasium to see its various basketball games, plays and graduations. By the time he finished a day behind the window in the post office, he usually had enough of the town doings—and also he cherished his quiet evenings in his upstairs apartment. A good cross word puzzle or a new issue of *National Geographic* was his fortification against local limitations.

As to talk of Roberta getting into the movies, he had to concede that things of that sort sometimes happened. Donna Belle Mullinger over in Denison had done it, getting some good roles in film and making a name for herself as a favorite pinup for the boys overseas who were fighting that damnable war. Of course, somebody had changed her name to "Donna Reed" which, it had to be admitted, had a more glamorous sound to it than "Mullinger."

In the spring, after the Senior class graduated, the Lotzberger family let it be known that Roberta had been approached by a talent scout who offered her the opportunity to take a screen test to see if she was movie star material. The family decided to allow that and even undertook to help Roberta choose a "stage" name for professional use. Thus, Roberta Lotzberger became "Lacy Jane White" before the very eyes of Millwell's citizens, most of whom—including Manny—wished her success. She then headed off for Hollywood in the care of a charming lady chaperone sent by MGM to supervise various young ingénues who were thought to have a future in films.

Nobody heard from her afterward, not even the young ministerial student who had taken advantage of his 4F classification to get a head start on a career and courting Roberta. Manny knew that she did write to her parents from time to time, because he put the letters into the Lotzberger mailbox, but the news must have been discouraging because the family didn't give out any updates. When the letters finally stopped coming, he felt for Roberta's/Lacy's mother and once, when she engaged him in conversation and admitted to him that "Lacy's" screen test hadn't resulted in any immediate offers of acting roles from the Hollywood crowd, he consoled her by telling her that most good things take time. Never, ever, did he tell anyone, including Doc, that Lacy/Roberta was a probable disappointment. His personal opinion was that she'd get a walk-on part in some low budget movie and then find another way to earn a living in California or come home to Millwell.

Nobody talked about it at all after a couple of years—assuming that if there was something exciting to report it would show up in

Millwell's weekly newspaper. The war in Europe ended and young men began coming home, good news indeed. Manny was kept busy stuffing wedding invitations and birth announcements into post office boxes. Hearing about which young man was going to sidestep his small town upbringing and head off for college on the G.I. bill was excitement enough. Who knew that John Malvern and Glen Olsen wouldn't join their fathers in the Malvern Garage and the Olsen Standard Oil gas station? Instead, even though neither young man had merited any attention for being a good student, with all the graduating honors in their classes going to young women, each apparently considered himself suited for a professional occupation and was headed off to Iowa City or Morningside College in Sioux City to prove it . Manny wished them well with all his heart. Would he, he reflected, be a small town postmaster if he'd had the advantage of a paid college education?

With all the new peacetime activities going on, Manny had his hands full. In addition to the usual social doings, there was a definite uptick in the amount of paid advertising. People could now buy things and lots of other people wanted to sell them things. The many advertisements and catalogs that poured in, all to be distributed via the post office, were overwhelming.

In mid-summer, Manny was mildly annoyed when a good-sized batch of colorful-looking brochures came in, each specifically addressed. Thumbing through them, he noticed that they were generally addressed to single men of relatively mature age. Some of these were so mature, in fact, that they were out pushing up daisies in the Millwell cemetery. One of the brochures was addressed to him, Manfred Streeter. Curious, he told Myrtle that he'd take care of distributing the junk mail himself, in the afternoon, and then he carried the brochure upstairs to his apartment to be read over his noontime bowl of chicken noodle soup.

What he saw when he broke the seal sent noodle soup spraying across his tidy kitchen table and surrounding floor. He had never seen such a thing. It was, indeed, an advertisement to send for more elaborate publications of the same kind, and what it was advertising were photos and short films of people, particularly young women, doing things that defied any possible activity seen by decent people. Manny knew the word "pornography" but had never heard it spoken aloud or had occasion to say it himself. Certainly, he had never seen

141

any, although back in his high school days someone had included him in the readership of a long, vulgar poem that had made his heart pound and his face turn red.

The mailing list for these brochures was evidently taken from some mysterious source that knew which Millwell men were single, mature, and possibly leading lives of sexual deprivation. Anger at the idea that he, Manfred Streeter, was included in that category inspired him to reflect on the entire situation. Not in his post office! By all the rules of heaven and hell, not in his post office!

Additionally, he did not think the United States of America would find such mail legal. He would destroy it before it got out to corrupt Millwell and Millwell's widowers and bachelors! He took one more good look to reinforce his indignation.

There were, of course, good looking young women—but women in various positions of having things done to them by men and even by other young women. All of them were buck naked. Additionally, there were men doing things to one another and a suggestion of extraneous objects and animals not ordinarily thought of in terms of human sexuality. Manny, who was well acquainted with the art galleries in Chicago and Washington, D. C., knew the Venus de Milo from Michelangelo's David. He was not a complete prude and had once considered buying some handsome books of world-famous art but found them too expensive. Of course, most of those nude figures in the art world were just standing there, definitely not engaged in the activities portrayed here. Perhaps because his standards were higher, he found the pictures in the brochure to be badly photographed as well as outrageous.

A block of type said that if the observer wanted more and better photos, even short films, they should send to box number 2159 in Kearney, Nebraska, enclosing the suggested payment.

Kearney, Nebraska! Manny hadn't troubled himself with traveling through Nebraska, having heard it was so flat that it made Iowa look like the Alps. This vulgar stuff was calling Kearney, Nebraska, home! Omaha or Lincoln might be believable; they were populous enough to harbor various forms of evil. But Kearney, an old Western town with few cosmopolitan pretensions to distinguish it?

Giving the brochure one more horrified look, Manny suddenly paused in amazement, almost lost his breathing capacity in fact. The face of one of the young women who was pictured was more clearly shown than some of the others since it was, at the moment, not buried in some portion of another person's anatomy. My God, it was Roberta Lotzberger, aka Lacy Jane White! It was her, it certainly was her! Had Manny not looked through the post office window at her throughout her growing years and seen her tossing her baton high in the air as she pranced at the head of the Millwell High School marching band? Roberta/Lacy, the disappointed movie starlet, was in Kearney, Nebraska, posing for pornography!

The first thing that must be done, Manny knew, was to get rid of all the brochures before one single other Millwell person saw them. They couldn't just be tossed in the trash; they would have to be burned. He went back downstairs to the post office and told Myrtle that the pile of brochures would all have to be returned to the sender due to insufficient postage and he would take care of it. She looked at him with a degree of puzzlement but he was the boss and it was nothing to her if he thought incoming mail had the wrong postage.

Manny piled the brochures in the closet space under the stairs and when the lobby closed for the day he retrieved them and carried them upstairs. It wasn't a Wednesday or Saturday so the stores weren't going to be open for the evening, a reason for gratitude. Around nightfall, when nobody seemed to be around, he hauled the nasty stuff down to the burn barrel that sat in the alley between the post office and the meat locker. Usually, he tried not to use it any more than necessary; a good stiff wind could send mischievous sparks flying into the air. In times of drought, there were local ordinances banning the use of open burning devices which made it a little hard to know what to do with personal papers that had to be thrown out. After all, they couldn't be taken to the dump as the owner of several of the downtown buildings did with cans and other miscellaneous garbage. This necessitated piling them up until a good day for burning presented itself.

Tonight, however, no drought had been declared and the wind was on the gentle side, at least for Iowa. Manny stuffed the brochures into the barrel, lit a match on each side of its opening, and stood watching as the flames crept up it sides. This was no casual matter, nosiree; he watched the fire consume every single scrap of paper, taking nothing for granted.

But, when he turned to make his way back up to his apartment he didn't have the sense of conclusion that he had anticipated. The thought that one of Millwell's own, Roberta Lotzberger, was out there in Kearney doing unspeakable things caused shivers to run down his spine. Was she perhaps being held against her will? Was someone or many someones threatening her life if she did not do the obscene things they photographed her doing?

It crossed his mind that, embarrassing as it would be to him personally, he should go to Roberta's parents, Millicent and Arnold Lotzberger, and tell them about their daughter. But, wait, maybe they wouldn't believe him. He should have kept one of the pornographic brochures to show them and he had not.

He dismissed the thought but wasn't surprised when a new resolve immediately replaced it. He, Manfred Streeter, would have to go to Kearney, Nebraska, and bring Roberta, aka Lacy Jane White, back to Millwell. There was no one else to do it—and no one else should know about it, now or in the future. It could be a dangerous mission. The kind of people that would have people pose so disgracefully would be likely to stop at nothing short of murder and he, Manny Streeter, could end up a good deal the worse for wear.

Shrugging his fears aside, he decided to go ahead with his plan.

"Can you give me a few extra days in the post office next week?" he asked Myrtle. "Something has come up and I need to take a couple of days off to tend to it."

Happy for the extra money, Myrtle was nonetheless coy and made a show of standing in front of the big wall calendar pondering. "I believe I can," she said, magnanimously. "I'll just push a couple of other things ahead for a few days."

The following Tuesday, around 7:00 a.m., Manny gassed up his tan Chevy and tossed an overnight bag into the trunk. He ate a big breakfast because Kearney wasn't a very long way from Millwell and he had no intention of stopping for lunch. Getting down to Omaha would take a little over an hour and Kearney was about four hours further west, a straight shot that would take him through the city of Lincoln where he could refill the gas tank.

Manny hadn't actually driven the route at any earlier time. Who wanted to waste their gas and time on a trip with so few rewards? The farm crops in Nebraska looked like the farm crops in Iowa and there were few sightseeing opportunities. If you wanted to be really honest about it, Nebraska didn't even have the bucolic look of Iowa, which at least had its slightly rolling hills. That over-rated Iowa artist, Grant Wood, likely hadn't looked twice at Nebraska!

Once over the Missouri River that ran between Council Bluffs and Omaha, the Platte River could be seen within sighting distance of the road. The Platte was of a piece with Nebraska, looking as thoroughly Midwestern as any stream could look. Flat. Wide. Stoic. Determined. Manny, who regularly drove with his eyes focused straight ahead, not even cutting himself any slack when, as now, there were very few cars on the road, occasionally found himself glancing over at the river. He had heard things about it serving as the trail landmark for pioneers heading toward Oregon or California, grateful for the shallow waters that allowed the easy crossing of covered wagons and animals. He had read somewhere else that a joke about the Platte had been formulated by some traveler: "Too thick to drink, too thin to plow," the gag went. One thing for sure; it wouldn't relieve anybody's boredom with the flat land that was Nebraska.

Manny got into Kearney early in the afternoon. The gas tank was again hovering on "low" and his stomach was growling. His foremost intent for the day was to get to the Kearney post office to, if possible, find out who had mailed the brochures that ended up in Millwell. Now, however, the Chevy needed to be gassed up and he needed to eat something. A fairly good sized station was just off the road and he pulled into it.

"Yessir?" said the kid who presented himself at the window on the driver's side.

"Fillerup," Manny said.

"Checkthaoil?" asked the kid.

"Yeah," said Manny. Ordinarily his instinct was to speak precisely and grammatically but he had learned years ago that there were times to take on the patterns of native speech. That should be easy for a person who had grown up in Des Moines, Iowa, but he just couldn't help his tendency to enunciate.

While the kid administered to the Chevy with gas nozzle, dipstick, and a windshield wiping contraption, Manny headed inside the station to use the rest room and see if any kind of food was available.

The restroom was clean but candy bars and pop were the only victuals available in the case beside the cash register. A woman, who was probably waiting for a tire to be fixed, stood looking out the station window and occasionally took a sip from the Pepsi-Cola bottle she held. Manny got a Baby Ruth candy bar from the man who was the cashier but who looked, considering his greasy overalls, as if his regular job might be in the little garage that adjoined the waiting room. Not one to strike up conversations with strangers, Manny let his eyes fall on the available reading material. He could have plucked a Nebraska map from the rack of maps beside the cash register but since he had no interest in driving beyond Kearney and, anyway, had a whole side pocket in the Chevy filled up with free maps of states he might or might not drive in the future, he looked at a thin newspaper that seemed to be a Kearney publication. Its headline said a group was going to meet on Wednesday to discuss the crane situation.

He must have looked puzzled and his forehead must have furrowed because the woman at the window looked at him and spoke up. Manny was immediately more comfortable because she looked and talked like the middle aged matrons who frequently stopped at his post office window to chat.

"You're not from around here, are you?" she said. "Does that Kearney headline surprise you?"

Manny nodded, prepared as always to listen.

"Every spring since the world was made," the woman said, "thousands and thousands of cranes come through here and settle for a couple of weeks on the Platte River just outside of Kearney. Some of us think it's important and there should be a celebration to honor it. It can be said that Kearney is the crane capital of the world."

The man in the greasy overalls grinned. "Nah," he said. "Kearney is the bird shit capital of the world. Some of us have to clean up after 'em."

The woman looked away; she'd heard the complaint before. Manny looked away, too. For one thing, such crudity in front of a lady was terrible. Also, "thousands and thousands of cranes" had a *National Geographic* feel to it, and he thought if he lived in Kearney he'd probably be on the woman's side of the argument. The Platte River had something important to offer, after all!

The cashier said, "Looks like your car's ready. Full tank, quart of oil, that'll be $4.10, plus a nickel for the candy bar."

Manny paid, tossed the Baby Ruth candy wrapper in a trash barrel, nodded to the pro-crane woman with the Pepsi, and went out to his car.

Downtown was not far away and Manny found the post office almost immediately. Three service windows in the lobby! Kearney must have eight to ten thousand inhabitants and there might be some kind of house to house delivery, not to mention at least three rural route delivery people. Manny stepped up to the middle window, which had a white-haired matron on duty and said, "I'd like to speak to the postmaster, if you please."

The woman stepped into the interior of the room and timidly rapped on a closed door, which then opened a crack. A fiftyish looking person with a grumpy face said, "Yeah?" Manny thought at first that the person was male and then looked harder. No, it was a woman—a woman who, in Doc Pinster language, looked "hard boiled." The lady with the white hair talked to the hard boiled woman in a soft voice, nodding in Manny's direction. The hard boiled woman, who was wearing what looked like a work shirt and a pair of men's pants, walked over to the service window.

"Yeah?" she said again. Evidently the word was her major mode of communication.

Manny tried hard to take on a hard boiled expression of his own. "Manfred Streeter," he said. He reached for his wallet, hoping he had some kind of identification that would look important. "I'm conducting an investigation into the use of second class mail."

The woman waved aside the identification that Manny held out. It was only his driver's license but perhaps she thought it was something else, something official that gave him the right to ask officious questions.

"Whatdayawannaknow?" she asked, maybe in tribute to Manny's starched white shirt and tie that he pretty much affected daily, the same way Doc Pinster always wore a white lab coat. He believed it made him look professional. That and his precise language.

Dene Hellman

"There are some questions being asked by several post offices," he said. "Some brochures have been coming in for distribution and we're told they include some unsavory content."

He thought the use of "we're told" was a nice touch. Only someone chosen to represent a "we" would have the credentials to bother regular people at work doing their dutiful best.

The woman ran a hand through her hair in thoughtful consideration. Her hair was cut quite short and evidently she wasn't in the least concerned about messing it up. Manny wasn't sure he'd ever seen a woman with that kind of haircut and hoped her credentials were proper.

"Betcha I know what you're talking about," she said. "Personally, I don't care what's in the brochures; people can do and see whatever they want. I can see, though, why some folks would get their panties in a twist."

Manny cringed, inwardly, while doing his best to keep a noncommittal face.

"Exactly!" he replied. He wasn't there to question the way people thought or spoke, or how they cut their hair, although he wondered if the postmistress was an appropriate representative of an honorable job. But all he really wanted was to get Roberta Lotzberger out of Kearney and home to Millwell.

The postmistress shrugged. "People who moved into Kearney last spring. I got no idea where they live. They got a post office box to collect their mail and paid for it. We don't ask people for their political views and religion of choice when they come in to mail something."

Manny knew the last sentence was thrown in as sarcasm and felt a little stung but declined to comment. The question that needed answering was where the stuff in the brochures was photographed. And by whom. And how to get Roberta away from their clutches. She might be a victim of white slavery! Manny didn't know quite what white slavery was, but it was a term that he occasionally read in news magazines and he assumed it meant women who were forced to do carnal things by criminals who had devious ways of keeping them captive.

He remained silent and did his best to retain a stern expression.

The postmistress evidently decided she would be as cooperative as possible, just in case this prissy looking man really had some kind of government authority.

"The post office box is in the name of "William Granada," she said. "That's all I know. The mail that comes in for him is addressed to 'Tropical Delights.' Kearney ain't no tropical delight, so maybe it's a business." Her face silently added the message, "Now get the hell out of my post office."

Manny removed himself from the building; the next step was to find a place to spend the night. He drove around a little, conscious that the tan Chevy was almost the only vehicle traveling down Kearney's residential streets. He saw an assortment of Victorian homes that had been built by prosperous people of the last century and a few newer ones that showed Tudor or colonial aspirations. Most streets, however, were lined with modest two-storied frame buildings that could use some fixing up.

Kearney didn't look any shabbier than most towns, considering that the war had gotten in the way of business-as-usual in the United States for several years and the Depression had curdled the economy for a long time before the war. Often, couples retired to town from work on their farms, perhaps leaving the farm houses and fields to the management of their offspring. The man would, at first, go out to the farm each day to help out. Then, as he aged, he might retire to one of the Main Street benches and put in a couple of years looking at people and vehicles that passed, conferring with other "loafers" who also were sidetracked to spectator status. Then he would get sick and die, leaving behind a spouse who might, if the home farm wasn't doing all that well, have to resort to penny-pinching. In larger towns, where strangers sometimes needed accommodations for a night or two, out would go a sign on the front window or lawn that said,

"Tourists Welcome."

Manny saw a tourist home sign on the front window of a house that looked a little more genteel than some others and directed the Chevy into its driveway. He knew very well that he was being observed by the lady of the house, as well as the occupants of nearby houses, so before he got out of the car he straightened his tie and did his best to tuck his shirt into his nicely pleated pants He rang the doorbell and said with great dignity to the elderly lady who answered, "I saw your sign that you have rooms to rent and I need one this evening. I've been in Kearney on business and would rather not head back to Council Bluffs tonight if it can be helped."

That got all his cards out on the table, even if some of the cards weren't quite accurate. The lady, who identified herself as Marjorie Finch, nodded understandingly and smiled. "Well, I'm sure I wouldn't want to start out driving in the middle of the afternoon, either! Are you alone? My rooms are nice and comfortable and you would have the upstairs hall bathroom to yourself, since I sleep downstairs."

Ah, the pleasure of a place where suspicion was not a cultivated attribute, thought Manny. Aloud, he said, "Thank you; I'm sure your room is all I could want or need. Just a moment and I'll get my overnight bag. Is my car okay where it is, or shall I move it?"

Once settled into his room, although he would like nothing better than to take a nice nap on the chenille bedspread that was evenly spread over the bed, Manny minded his manners. Sneaking a look at the pillows that were encased in the top of the spread, he found they were, just as he expected, very clean, plump and down-filled. The pillow slips were embroidered in blue flossed depictions of Dutch girls with watering cans; it would be sacrilegious to take them out of their chenille tombs and lay one's head on them before a proper time when all good people were settling for the night. Anyway, he would have to find someplace to eat and do some research before he could think of resting.

"Do you have plans for dinner?" asked his hostess, who had come up the stairs to bring him towels.

"Not really," Manny said. "If you can recommend an eating place, I'll be most appreciative."

The lady said, so sure was she of the gentility of her roomer, "If you can put up with modest fare, you are welcome to have dinner with me. My brother said he might come by so we wouldn't be alone." The last was added, Manny was sure, to show that the hospitality wasn't being offered in the spirit of a tete-a-tete. He accepted the invitation gratefully, wondering whether one offered to pay for one's meal or just quietly tacked some sort of gratuity on to the room rent.

Deciding to go with the pretense of the meal being free, when he paid for his room he would add two dollars to the cost. Mrs. Finch would demure, and he would say, "You are so kind. Please allow me to show my gratitude for such lovely accommodations." At the moment, he just hoped that dinner would be served sooner rather than later.

Having made a decision as to what would be a good time to eat, Mrs. Finch knocked gently on the door of Manny's room at twenty minutes past five. "Wash hands!" she said with a gaiety that signified friendliness. "We'll have dinner in ten minutes!"

Manny's Aunt Pricilla would have served exactly the same thing to an unexpected guest: salmon loaf made from canned salmon, sliced tomatoes from the garden, scalloped potatoes, homemade dill pickles, freshly made pineapple upside down cake, all on an ironed tablecloth plus cloth napkins that were probably retrieved from a seldom-used linen closet. The china was surely the lady's best set. Manny knew that he was expected to provide conversation, information and opinions that could be later relayed to his hostess's friends. It wasn't every day that she rented her room to such a proper gentleman!

He asked about the cranes.

"They really are a sight," said his hostess. "Hundreds of thousands of them and they come from all over the world to spend time here in Kearney. It's mostly cranes but there are some geese and migrating birds among them."

Manny said that must be quite a spectacle.

Mrs. Finch said she had gone out to see them a couple of times, over the years.

"I just wish they'd pick some other time of year to do their traveling," she said. "It's always late February to early April and you know what our Midwestern weather is at that time. I just about froze my feet off both times I went."

She asked, tactfully, about Manny's occupation, place of residence, and did he have a family? Manny said, more or less truthfully and very carefully, "Oh, kind of an investigative government job. I come from Des Moines, Iowa, and haven't met anyone yet that I'm ready to settle down with."

His hostess nodded in an understanding way, her face taking on a relatively animated expression when he said he hadn't met anyone to settle down with. She was likely going over in her head, immediately, which Kearney lady noted for her lovely personality and respectable availability she could match him up with. He decided to cut that off at the roots and try to extract some useful information from *her*.

Making a show of hesitating, he then said, almost in hushed tones, "I'm actually in Kearney looking for some folks of interest to the authorities. Do you know of any newcomers to the area who've settled here in the last few months? I'm not talking families, exactly. Just a bunch of folks who might have started up a business?"

He mimed a finger across his lips in a wartime "Do you know who's listening?" gesture. The lady was immensely and immediately flattered and Manny could tell she was going to oblige him with everything she knew or had even considered.

"So funny you should ask that," she said. "There are always a few newcomers but most of them are just like an open book. I've kind of wondered about this one outfit that's rented the house and outbuildings at the old Reed place. A friend and I pass the farm on Sundays when we drive out to the country church we attend."

Manny knew better than to assume anything. "Don't the owners need the buildings?" he asked.

"Oh, goodness, no," said Mrs. Finch. "The Reeds own a bunch of farms and remodeled the house on one of them into a regular mansion. The house on the farm I'm talking about is quite nice, but wasn't good enough for the Reeds since they've become so prosperous. And the barn is huge, big enough for any kind of hobby. I do hope the renters aren't up to any kind of mischief. When we passed by last Sunday, I noticed one of those big old station wagons standing in the driveway and a couple of big panel trucks close to the barn."

Aha! Manny said to himself. Aloud, he said, "Mrs. Finch, I don't have any idea if the people who are living there are the ones I'm looking for—but I certainly will investigate. Will you be so kind as to give me directions to the farm?"

Mrs. Finch was obviously thrilled and she, in turn, put her index finger to her lips in Uncle Sam mode and then drew him a little diagram on a piece of scratch paper. Getting to the Reed place wouldn't be complicated, according to the crude map.

She nodded with understanding when Manny suggested that he had a long day of driving and would have another one tomorrow, so did she mind if he excused himself and went to his room to do a little planning and to get a good night's sleep? If convenient, he would like to check out in the morning around 9:00.

It was a bit hard to break away when he was ready to depart. Mrs. Finch insisted that Manny have a tiny bit of breakfast, that it came with the room rental, and that it would be her pleasure. Manny acquiesced, then added another dollar to the sum he handed her when he left, quickly ducking her protestations. As he waved from the driveway, he could see her mouth working and when he rolled down the window to hear, made out the words, "Now you come back—and bring that special someone you will surely find very soon!"

The directions were surprisingly simple. It was a matter of driving down one gravel road, going left at the second stop sign, then right on the next gravel road for several miles, then looking for a white house on the left side that was set back unusually far from the road. The house would have a barn close behind it. It was hard to say if the mailbox would provide any information but maybe there would be a couple of panel trucks in the yard that had names painted on them.

Manny reached his destination quickly and debated whether to turn into the driveway or leave the Chevy along the road. He compromised, deciding to go up the drive to the house but only for a short distance, just in case it was necessary to make a quick getaway. He felt his mouth go dry. What was the next move?

Logically, when he collected his wits, the next move was to go the farmhouse and knock on the door; if one was selling Watkins vanilla or handing out religious tracts, that's what one would do. Manny got out of the Chevy, trying for a nonchalant look on his face, making the routine move to tuck his shirt into his pants and straighten his tie before marching resolutely toward the door.

But getting as far as the door wasn't necessary after all because a man came around the side porch and walked toward him. A youngish man, maybe mid-thirties, crew cut, dressed in denim pants and a faded short-sleeved sport shirt. He looked like one of the Millwell guys who worked in the lumber yard and Manny relaxed a bit. Had he been expecting horns and cloven hooves?

"Lost?" asked the man in quite a respectable voice.

"Oh, I don't need directions," said Manny. "I've been told this is where I might be able to find somebody I know."

The man looked skeptical. "I doubt it," he said, and looked meaningfully at Manny's tie and pleated pants. He sat down on one of the front porch steps and jerked his thumb toward another one, indicating that Manny should likewise sit. "Bill Granada," he said, holding out his hand to shake—a gesture Manny thought fit to ignore.

"It happens," Manny began, choosing his words carefully, "that I've been asked to look into the disappearance of a young woman from Millwell."

Did he sound official? Would he have to do the fake government thing, suggesting that he was on the payroll of the FBI? This individual, with his deliberately blank face, looked as if he didn't care who Manny represented. Maybe he was being figured as a private investigator? Well, that would do; anything that set him aside from a low-level busybody.

"I expect you'd know her as Lacy White," he added.

The young man's expression didn't change. "Ah, Lacy," he said. "What do you want to do about her?"

"Take her home to her folks," said Manny. There! It was out; no pretenses of any kind asked for or given.

"Not a bad idea," said the Bill person. "Frankly, she's a lousy actress and we were going to have to let her go in the next couple of months. Hard telling where she'd end up but those are the breaks."

Actress? *Actress*? Is that what they called the obscene performances sold through the mail? Evidently so. Even the scum of the earth had its euphemisms, Manny thought. And even as he turned that idea over in his mind, here came Roberta/Lacy up toward the house from the barn, with one hand holding a skimpy robe semi-closed over her obviously unclothed self.

"Mr. Streeter!" she said, when she caught sight of Manny sitting on the porch steps beside the man who was, likely, her boss.

Half rising from his perch, Manny couldn't think of anything to say, but the Bill Granada guy spoke directly. "Lacy, go get some clothes on. This guy says he's taking you home."

Without another word, Lacy/Roberta hoisted herself up on the porch and went through the front door, slamming it behind her. Granada looked at Manny. Since Lacy had greeted him with a startled, "Mr. Streeter!" Manny's role appeared a bit less evident. He could be anybody who had crossed Lacy's path. Manny squirmed inwardly. When Granada said, courteously if you will, "While you're waiting, would you like to go over to the barn and watch some of the filming?" Manny was embarrassed beyond description. He found himself getting red, then felt a kind of total shrinking settle down through the pit of his stomach.

"Ah, no. We got to get going." Following those words, he was on his feet, down the driveway and into his Chevy in what seemed like one semi-levitated move.

There wasn't long to wait. Roberta came down the drive wearing a skimpy pair of shorts and a midriff-baring top, carrying nothing but a teeny little handbag. She opened the car door and slid into the front seat on the passenger side. Manny expected that she'd ask some questions and he'd have to provide reassurance of some kind but the girl turned her head away. Manny backed out onto the gravel road. Neither of them said anything until they reached the outskirts of Kearney.

"Do you need something to eat?" Manny asked. He had no idea in the world what else to say. Roberta shook her head and once the car was on the highway she broke into loud sobs accompanied by much sniffling and—after Manny passed her his handkerchief— much nose blowing.

And so it went, through Nebraska to the outskirts of Lincoln. The Chevy's gas tank was dangerously low so a stop had to be made. Both Manny and Roberta went to their respective rest rooms and Manny was a little worried when he had to wait quite some time for Roberta to emerge. When she did, he was relieved to see that she had washed her face, applied some lipstick and combed her hair. While she didn't look like the Roberta Lotzberger who had led the Millwell marching band down Main Street a couple of years before, had in fact aged several years from that time, she still was a young woman who could turn heads. In proof of that, the guy who had filled the gas tank and washed the windshield lingered on, swiping at little invisible places, taking his own sweet time getting over to the next vehicle waiting for service.

On the road again, Manny thought it was time to get some things straight and addressed Roberta with a plan he had developed on the silent drive from Kearney. "Look," he said, "I'm not going to drive you farther than Omaha. We'll go as far as downtown and you call your folks to come pick you up. Tell them you were coming home and got a ride as far as Omaha with some friends. Don't mention me, now or later. Ever. I found something out and came after you but that's a secret that you and I need to carry to our graves."

This was met with silence and, a few moments later, he added, "You should get a sandwich or soup or something and if you're smart you'll buy a dress to wear home."

Roberta's reply was short. "No money," she said.

Arriving at Omaha's commercial district, Manny reached for his wallet and extracted a twenty. "This ought to cover lunch and a decent dress and the phone call," he said.

The girl stuck the money into her teeny purse and when he let her out in front of a big downtown department store, she jumped out of the car with a hint of her old baton-twirling ease.

"Thanks," she said as she slammed the door closed.

He never saw her again.

That she was safely home in the bosom of her family was certain since Mrs. Lotzberger was in the post office as often as usual and sometimes stopped at the lobby window to visit. Manny wouldn't, for all the world, ask about Roberta but her mother volunteered information now and then. It was certain that she knew nothing of what Manny had done because her story, for all of Millwell to know, was that Roberta had decided to forego a contract and other movie star amenities as a result of finding the Hollywood scene much too immoral for her finely-tuned Iowa sensibilities.

In September, the news was that Roberta had gone to the teachers' college in Cedar Falls to work on a certificate in rural education and a year later the news was that her former boyfriend had been ordained and was an assistant pastor in a church in Waterloo. In March, Mrs. Lotzberger shared the happy news that Roberta would marry her young minister the following June. It would be a big wedding and it would be in Millwell.

Late in April, a huge pile of wedding invitations was delivered to the Millwell post office and all the ensuing postal chores required a phenomenal amount of effort. Manny spent extra time inserting all the invitations very neatly into the post office boxes, looking carefully at the addresses as he moved around.

Doc Pinster got one, of course, as did everyone else who had ever rendered any service to one of the Lotzbergers. All of the local business people got one. Every former teacher of Roberta's whose whereabouts was known got one.

Of all the people in town, he ruefully discovered, he was the only respectably employed person who did not receive an invitation to the wedding. And after he had been ready to risk his life to extract Roberta/Lacy from the terrible circumstances in which he found her!

"Ah, well," he said to himself. "At least I won't have to come up with some excuse as to why I can't attend."

THE EMBEZZLER

THE HEADLINE, ONE OF MANY that would display over several weeks before petering out in an indecisive finale, identified the woman as Debra Klein, whose light fingers had supposedly peeled tens of thousands of dollars, perhaps as much as $300,000, from the coffers of Rathmore City's Righteous Way Fellowship of Believers.

Rodney Pilcher, the junior clergyman of Righteous Way's roster of reverends, told the Rathmore City Courier, "We held Ms. Klein in the highest regard for the twenty-three years she was on our staff, and are shocked and sorrowful beyond words. It's hard to imagine how we could have been more generous and welcoming. Sadly, the money she took could have done so much for those people who hunger and thirst after God's presence in their lives. Even so, as always, our cloak of forgiveness and love is wrapped around her and her family."

The cloak of forgiveness and love didn't extend, at first, to the point of not pressing charges. However, an absence of proof as to the amount of shortfall in the Righteous Way's coffers, as well as a fear of scaring off future contributors, sent the situation bumping up against a dead end. A heartbreaking sermon in which The Reverend Mr. Orville Pilcher wept about the joys of granting mercy was his last pubic word about the crime.

The Klein family thought it best to move away from Rathmore City—even from the state—in an effort to hide from disgrace. Debra's husband, Jerry, chided her for a year or two for what she had done.

"What didja do with the rest of it?" he demanded. When Debra finally convinced him that she had taken nothing close to the $300,000 suggested, and that what she had stolen had been spent on family needs, he demanded a divorce and went back to Rathmore City proclaiming his own innocence of the whole sordid affair.

The children were young adults and deeply resentful at having their reputations sullied by their mother's moral mistakes. The daughter, married a year or so before in a ceremony that was quite nice by Rathmore City's unassuming standards, was especially angry. "You could have disgraced me before I even got married," she declared. "Then nobody would have given us any presents or come to the wedding!"

Within a year, the kids did what they would have done anyway; they followed their opportunities and inclinations to different venues.

Debra's mother, Maybelle, was too far along in years to move away from her comfortable assisted living quarters but told everyone who would listen, as long as she lived, that she had always been apprehensive about her daughter's capacity to reject temptation. "Even as a little girl," she said, " she always wanted more than her share and would sneak an extra cookie any time she thought I wasn't looking. Maybe she is one of them 'bad seeds' they talk about."

Debra was left alone to brood and pray. Food stamps helped put food on her table but she would likely have become homeless if Sharon, a former friend from high school, hadn't taken her in at the last moment to help with the cottages she rented out to summer visitors.

Sharon heard another side of the story from Debra and that's the one that now prevails.

In 1990, when Debra first went to work for The Righteous Way Fellowship of Believers, there were not all that many Believers. Rodney Pilcher's father, Orville, was the head clergyman and he'd been at it for a couple of decades, using his beautiful baritone to half sing, half preach his way into the consciousness of some of the Rathmore City folks.

Occasionally, therefore, he was asked to give the opening prayer at the town council meetings but otherwise wasn't particularly acknowledged. The Fellowship held services in a shabby one-room hall that had been outgrown by the local Jehovah's Witnesses. The town Methodists, Lutherans and Congregationalists ignored him. "Who ordained him?" they asked one another, and since Orville's credentials were underwhelming and his origins were traceable to Missouri hill country, they put him and his church down on their lists of socially questionable institutions.

Orville kept on singing and that, plus nice sermons that were heavy on the forgiveness angle, especially forgiveness for sins ordinary folks could understand—not complicated activities, like "coveting" that, unspecified, brought the Lutherans to their communion rails—he gained a following of those same ordinary folks.

Before anybody in higher Rathmore City social circles noticed, the Righteous Way Fellowship had built a rather nice looking church on the grounds they already inhabited.

Orville's son, Rodney, now in his mid-twenties, was welcomed into the pulpit to preach and sing beside his father, and the pair, father and son, pleaded with their congregation to make even better things happen. More people could be saved!

Unlike the well-bred pastors of Rathmore's traditional denominations, the Pilchers did not hold periodic campaigns to agitate for bigger contributions and tithes. "God loves yah!" was their continuous cry. "Be healed! Make a joyful noise unto the Lord! Give what you can to further His work and know that He is Lord!"

Wow! Sunday contributions increased exponentially as well-folded bills were thrust into the passed collection basket, arriving straight from dormant spells in tea pots and tool boxes, rededicated from their original goals as the down payment on a sofa or a motorcycle.

"Somebody needs to count it," said the Pilchers to one another, preferring to spend their time buffing up their star quality with sermons and songs and confidence that they now had a good formula for bringing in cash.

"It's not what you'd call a tough job," they said to Debra when she applied to be their accountant. "Couple of days a week, maybe. You keep track of the money, make out a deposit slip, then give the donations to one of us to take to the bank."

The Pilchers proved how easy they thought the job would be by offering the current minimum wage — $3.80 an hour. Debra accepted, hoping to do her job so well that she'd be offered more before a lot of time passed.

Minimum wages were up to $4.25 an hour the next year, so that was sort of a raise, and the Pilchers were offering her five days a week of employment by 1992. The collection plates brimmed over, she counted the cash, and Mrs. Rodney Pilcher, who had brought her big blue eyes and expansive bust size into the pulpit shortly after marrying Rodney, took over doing the bank deposits. Mrs. Pilcher had a lovely singing voice and could proclaim, "God LOVES yah!" with great sincerity. Debra sometimes wondered who was paying for the lady's gorgeous wardrobe, but assumed it was coming out of the salaries of the Mr. Pilchers, Senior and Junior. Make that Doctor Pilcher, Senior, because that title suddenly began attaching itself to the older man. Who was to say that it wasn't valid?

In 1997, The Righteous Way Fellowship bought air time on the radio—which they said they should have thought to do before—and the three Pilchers sang and preached their ways over the airwaves into the hearts of many, many people in an entire six state region who longed to be assured God loved them, despite their relative shortcomings. Brimming collection plates were no longer the name of the game; envelopes now came in the mail from listeners and brought steady cash. Debra couldn't get it all counted by herself so a small staff of women was employed to slit the envelopes open, record the amount in each, and list the names and addresses of the senders for future solicitation. The Pilchers gave Debra the title Lead Accountant and raised her hourly pay to $6.50, which was more than a dollar above the minimum wage the new women received.

Also, she was moved into a tiny, windowless office of her own, presumably to shield from prying eyes the volume of cash once all of the envelopes' contents were put together.

A large and stylish church was begun on the former Jehovah Witness grounds while the somewhat older structure was designated as the office building. The Pilchers were really hitting their strides and by the turn of the century they made it to television. Young Reverend Rodney Pilcher added a doctorate designation to his name and was thereby no longer outclassed by his father. His wife didn't seem to yet be doctorate material but her blue eyes, fabulous figure and smoky brown hair began to be seen in the weekly grocery store magazines and talk shows. Her expertise, it seemed, was in more than looking wonderful; she was able to talk at length about how pureness of heart and devotion to one's spouse did so much for one's appearance. She even wrote a little book encouraging women to make the most of their looks by adopting her own brand of false eyelashes and shampoo while cleaving unto their husbands with loving respect; before long, she had a small following of her own, most of whom felt assured that somebody, even if not necessarily God, would shortly love them.

Minimum wage was still $5.15 an hour when the new century began so Debra couldn't get beyond $6.50. There were more counters of cash than ever so she had more to do but when she tried to talk to one of the Pilchers about it, they pointed out that she had taken a month of maternity leave early in the 1990s and another one a couple of years later. In both cases, they said, they had gladly held her job for her. They also told her that God loved her, a statement that was beginning to wear rather thin since God didn't provide much evidence of appreciation.

For one thing, Jerry, her husband, was an on again, off again worker. A bit of a drinker, he tended to lose track of time and subsequently fail to clock in at various factory jobs, which often put him back among the unemployed. Debra's work at Righteous Way Fellowship was increasingly important. It kept the family relatively solvent even though Debra was, by now, ready to scream with boredom. Cash had stopped having any edge to it so, as she watched the women in the large mail room slit open their envelopes and pile the enclosed offerings into stacks that would later be turned over to her, it was no more relevant than seeing Monopoly money in games played by her kids. When she collected it and verified it, made out deposit slips in triplicate, then gave it to Mrs. Rodney Pilcher to bank, she was without any sense of having done a task with discernible value.

Early in the new century, Debra discovered romance novels. They were everywhere, disseminated by all manner of publishers, including self-publishing companies, and online entities that she couldn't begin to define. Often rife with misspellings, typos and grammatical errors, they poured forth into the eager hands of women who spent a small fortune each week to read about the satisfactions of love lost, mourned and finally requited. Debra spent a lot of her free time canvassing the shelves of drugstores and mega groceries for new books and was successful often enough to give some pleasure to lunch periods and the lulls between money counting. When there were no new romances to be read, she reread the old ones.

Jerry's teeth, never in very good shape, began aching enough to cast a shadow over their lives and she at first wondered what to do. He was her husband and his moaning and sleepless nights because of his many decaying and broken molars and incisors caused her great worry. They had no insurance, medical or dental, no savings, and no prospects. What could be done?

The solution that occurred to her was as elementary as figuring out the water temperature for a load of laundry. She felt little or no emotion the day she began to slip bills, five and ten dollar bills when available, between the pages of her current romance novel. Each day, she took the book of the day home and shook it empty of the money into a shoe box that was tucked toward the back of their hall closet, well behind the debris of winter hats. When she finally decided to count it, it added up to about $5,000. She told Jerry that she had been saving a little money for the children's Christmas and some new linoleum for the kitchen floor and thought there was enough so he could go see a dentist. He chided her for holding out on him but accepted the cash without question as no more than his due. The dentist's fees absorbed all of it and, in time, Jerry had dentures instead of pain and was easier to live with.

In retrospect, Debra felt remorse for her thievery and worried where she would get the money to pay back Righteous Way. This was obscured by a sort of mental block, but as a reader of romance novels she knew that good things often happen unexpectedly and went back to her days of blameless counting and tabulating contribution money, then turning all of it over to Mrs. Rodney Pilcher for deposit.

A formal accounting department had been put in place sometime before. The gentleman who was hired to head it was paid an unknown amount of money but it probably was tremendously more than Debra received because he drove a nice, late model car, wore a necktie, and had an air of professional competence. He went to lunch with the Pilchers from time to time and even joined them on various ski vacations and during the crusades they now held in cities across the continent. Money was coming in from sources other than the personal envelopes sent by converts to the people whose sermons and songs insisted that God loved them. This was the money that he—and assistants he hired—took care of. To all appearances, it was *important* funding and Debra's particular source, i.e. the personal envelopes, seemed to accrue only to Mrs. Rodney Pilcher—who was, by now, making little speeches about funding for young women's education in the domestic sciences. This kind of emphasis for young women, she told the world, would be the salvation of families, thereby coaxing them to traditional lives of service to their husbands and children. A lot of older women bought into this objective and made it a point to add a dollar or two to their offerings whenever possible.

Maybelle, Debra's mother, was widowed a couple of years after Jerry's teeth were taken care of. The husband who passed on was her second spouse and not Debra's father. He had been ailing for much of the marriage and consequently was of limited social and domestic use, but had brought with him, when they married, a pension from years as the widower of a government employee. When he died, the pension died. Stricken with grief and chagrin, Maybelle wept loudly to Debra about what would become of her in her newly acquired poverty. Debra reluctantly, because Maybelle was hard to get along with, offered her mother a home with her. Maybelle refused, swearing that Jerry's alcohol habits were not in tune with her own Christian lifestyle, that the children were noisy, and that she needed more personal care than Debra had time to give. She needed, she said, to take up residence in a local retirement home, Senior Friends, that was dedicated to elderly Christian folks of good habits.

Entrance costs were almost $25,000 so the most Debra could say was, "Give me a little time to try to raise the money, Ma. Maybe I can get a loan from the credit union where we bank."

Without collateral, that was a big joke and Debra went back to sliding money between the pages of whatever romance novel she was reading. Television land remained generous, with folks from modest walks of life sending in their contributions along with notes of appreciation and/or tales of woe.

Debra supposed wealthier folks were donating money in other ways, money that would be recorded and acknowledged by the Righteous Way's more important fiscal management, but the team of women who slit open envelopes had been enlarged several times. To keep everyone honest, overhead cameras now swept the room where they worked.

The minimum wage went up to $6.55 in 2008 and, subsequently, Debra's hourly pay was raised to $8.00. She didn't think that was very generous for 18 years of monotonous work but Mrs. Rodney Pilcher, to whom she applied for an enhanced salary, told her that she was very fortunate to have such a dependable and important employer, as well as having a small office of her own, and should count her blessings. "We just have to be so very frugal in order to meet our wonderful goals," she explained, giving a little flip to her pleated cashmere skirt.

Debra found enough non-incentive in Mrs. Pilcher's remarks to increase the amounts that came to rest between the pages of her books. Additionally, she found another way to siphon off cash; she became a continuous drinker of colas. Since many people were thus addicted and always had a can in hand or in front of them, this was relatively easy. She brought the cans from home and made sure that each had been discreetly opened around the edge and its contents dumped. Thus, she only pretended to drink, instead filling each can with cash. Sometimes she was amazed that nobody caught on, but since she had never made any close friends at the Righteous Way Fellowship of Believers, nobody paid attention. She could go just about any place, from home to work to grocery store, with a can of cola in her hand and nobody even noticed.

Within a year, Debra had an amount of money in hand that she could turn over to the Senior Friends for Maybelle's admission. Of course, Maybelle would have to give the Friends nearly all of her monthly Social Security income, plus other government contributions available for her care, in order to remain eligible for residency so Maybelle told Debra that she would now need to depend upon her for spending money.

"I gotta get my hair fixed every week," she said. "Plus, Senior Friends get taken to a bunch of local activities and surely you don't want me setting home while everybody else is out having a good time."

Jerry was plenty aggravated, not to mention mystified about the whole thing. "How come you never said you could get your hands on that kinda money?" he asked. "I coulda used a fishing boat or we coulda got a camper and had some fun."

Debra declared that she had obtained a loan for Maybelle's

entrance fees and would have to pay it back bit by bit.

"Huh!" said Jerry. "You must be holdin' out some way."

After that he told everybody, including his relatives, "That Debra's a real whiz with money. She can make it stretch farther than a rubber band on steroids. Acourse, we're all payin' for it in other ways. She don't seem to care what we're all doin' without!"

The kids took what their dad said to heart and when it was time to get jobs and leave home they didn't exhibit any ambition for moving on.

Then Debra's daughter, Sarah, decided to get married and made it known that she wanted a wedding that was better than, or at least the equal of, that of her previously married friends. She drove Debra crazy with wedding magazines and endless trips to department stores to decide what she would register as necessary trappings for her future and glorious life with Rafe, as soon as he got out of the Army. Debra didn't even know about Lenox china and Waterford glass, had never possessed much of anything with more illustrious beginnings than Walmart, and thought it was all a bunch of hooey. Still, she didn't want to break her daughter's heart and so went along with it. Rafe wasn't due for release from the Army for about six months but deposits had to be made and a gown purchased and there were other costs that amazed her. What had happened to getting into a car with a license in one's pocket and one's intended by one's side and just going over the nearest town and doing it? Evidently, despite a significant decrease in the middle class, that kind of thing was passé.

She didn't have much time. By now, layering money between the pages of a book and/or stuffing it into coke cans was as boring as every other aspect of her job. Adding sums up, she figured she must owe the Righteous Way Fellowship about $40,000, maybe even $45,000.

Mrs. Rodney Pilcher, the leading light in the domesticity crusade, continued to pick money up from Debra at least twice a week, taking it and the deposit slips Debra made out with careful penmanship to the bank. Debra filed the third copy of each deposit slip in a drawer and never looked at it again and never saw any of the ensuing paperwork.

She assumed the more important accounting department took it from there. Sometimes she wondered if there was a camera trained on her, just as it was on the women in the larger room, but nobody seemed greatly interested in what she did, beyond filling out deposit slips and hanging on to the envelope money until Mrs. Rodney Pilcher took it off her hands.

The wedding funds came along efficiently. Debra told herself that *nobody*, not even her daughter, needed a wedding that cost more than $10,000, so when that amount had been achieved, Debra quit squirreling away money. Her daughter's wedding was pleasant, she thought, but the rest of the family complained that it made them look stingy. Maybelle was the most annoyed at the various little economies.

"You should of got somebody in to do hair for all of us the morning of the ceremony!" she said. "And I was ashamed to tell my acquaintances at Senior Friends that I had to wear the same dress to the rehearsal dinner and the wedding."

Lying awake nights wondering how she was going to make up the shortfall she'd caused to the Fellowship, Debra began to buy lottery tickets with some of the money she'd previously dedicated to romance novels but she never won anything. She sent Publisher Sweepstakes entries back as fast as they came in, hardly expecting to win but thinking one really never knew, did one?

Her son had graduated from high school the year before, which was a blessing considering his lack of enthusiasm for studying, and when he said it wasn't fair to give his sister that much money just for a wedding when he could use a new truck, she told him to do like all the rest of the poor guys and sign on with Uncle Sam.

"You can get an education that way," she told him. "That's a double blessing. You serve your country and get a lifetime of payback. I wish somebody had told me that when I was your age."

She felt bad saying those words, knowing it was another kind of lottery that her son would be entering, one that had a life or death outcome, but she couldn't bring herself to take more money from the Righteous Way Fellowship of Believers.

In the end, it was Debra's worry and her resolve to quit taking money that did her in. When she went into the big room where the women sat slitting open the contribution envelopes, her body language began to look *different*. Somehow, she just looked as if she wanted to disappear into herself. The overhead cameras picked it all up, including the worried look on her face, and the people in the important accounting department began to notice. One or two of them stopped her and asked if she was feeling okay and that made her shrink even more.

The head accountant dropped by her office one day and asked for her deposit slips from the prior year. She had the duplicate of everything she'd given Mrs. Rodney Pilcher and willingly turned those over. After all, they were accurate representations of the cash she had passed on.

Since she was required to keep no formal accounts beyond the deposit slips, there were none of the elaborate ledgers that mainstream embezzlers are said to juggle. The money she had stolen was never known by anyone but her to exist. The only other person to see the cash from the contribution envelopes was Mrs. Pilcher and she had never exhibited the slightest tendency to question what Debra put in her hands.

In less than a week, the head of the accounting department confronted Debra with an emphatic statement that she had been caught red-handed. It turned out that during the times when Debra was on the take, larding her romance novels and filling her cola cans with contribution cash, smaller totals were being listed on the deposit slips than at other times. Additionally, much of the time the deposit slips didn't agree with the amounts of cash that actually were deposited. The bank's records showed different deposits altogether than what was on Debra's copies.

"The inconsistency is staggering!" the accountant said. "I don't know how you did it, but there's a fortune missing and you will have to answer to it."

He made a call and Debra was arrested. Since her family didn't know what to say or do, it was Debra herself who thought to ask for a lawyer. Fortunately for her, the attorney seemed to be a skeptical sort and when Debra acknowledged to him that she may have taken some money but not the hundreds of thousands that were being talked about, and she'd used what she took to take care of family needs because her salary was so very low, he listened carefully.

"Ha!" he said. "Wouldn't put anything past those hypocrites over there. They let you sit in a room by yourself for years and years without any formal justification for why you answered to only one person. You were a pawn, my dear. You could have gone on dipping into the pie until the day you retired, and nobody would have investigated. They may even have expected it. Mrs. Tinker Bell, or whatever her name is, was the real embezzler and it was so damn easy when you gave her the cash. She simply made out new deposit slips for a lot less. I'd bet my law degree on it."

Then he went to see the Pilchers, father, son and lovely wife, and that was when they quickly decided to drop the charges against Debra. There were earnest and public prayers for her but of course she was out of a job and wouldn't be able to get another one. Her function as tabulator of unofficial contribution funds was completely absorbed into the formal accounting department and Mrs. Rodney Pilcher, who was looking quite chastened, was not only eliminated as a depositor of cash but disappeared from the pulpit and the airways for nearly six months. It was said that she was unwell, worn out from her many activities on behalf of young women's domestic responsibilities and also that she hoped to soon begin a family.

After Debra's family abandoned her—a logical outcome for her thieving ways—and her high school friend had taken her in to help with summer renters, it took months before she was able to return to any semblance of her former self. Mostly, after her work was done, she sat silently in corners, staring into space. Sometimes she reached into her piles of romance novels and read for an hour or two.

"You really like that stuff, don't you?" asked Sharon, her chum and benefactor.

"Oh, yes," said Debra "They're all about real people and real things that happen to them and everything comes out for the best."

"Could people who don't have a college degree write one?" asked the friend.

Debra thought about that. Sometimes she had scribbled notes in a notebook she had picked up at Target. "I guess so," she said, thinking of the little plot ideas that sometimes came to her and that she had jotted down. "I'm not real well educated but I suppose we women have a lot of stuff in common."

A month or so later, she asked Sharon if she could use her computer for a few hours a week, and permission was granted.

"Looking up from her desk, Lisa saw the most gorgeous man she had ever beheld," went the opening line of a document that

became Debra's first romance novel.

Writing them was almost as good as reading them. Debra had a knack, a way of getting to the heart of things and choosing words to convey angst, seduction and ultimate grace that made women hasten to buy her books. In not too long, she grew prosperous and well-known, and knew that she was a real success the day she took a check for $45,000 over to the headquarters of the Righteous Way Fellowship of Believers.

She presented it to the head accountant and was careful to get a return receipt.